CROSSING THE LINE

KTS #2

ELISE FABER

CROSSING THE LINE
BY ELISE FABER
Newsletter sign-up

CROSSING THE LINE
Copyright © 2021 Elise Faber
Print ISBN-13: 978-1-63749-000-6
Ebook ISBN-13: 978-1-946140-99-9
Cover Art by Jena Brignola

KTS SERIES

Prequel Novella
Fire and Ice (Hurt Anthology)

Full Length Books
Riding The Edge
Crossing The Line (March 22nd, 2021)
Leveling The Field (June 14th, 2021)

CHAPTER ONE

KTS Satellite Base
Western Georgia
16:22hrs

Olive

I STRODE DOWN THE HALL.

Okay, maybe I *stomped* down the hall.

Mostly because of the man at my back.

He was absolutely infuriating.

Case in point, him coming up behind me, grabbing my arm, and turning me to face him. I could have jerked away, could have knocked him on his ass, but my biggest weakness as an agent for the private military operation, KTS, was also my best attribute as a doctor.

I didn't like hurting people.

Even when they wanted to hurt me. Sure, I would do it if necessary. I *could* definitely do it if the circumstances required—if my life or the life of my fellow agents or the life of an innocent were threatened.

But I really hated it.

Which was why I simply glared at the infuriating man known as Linc when he yanked me to a halt and growled, "Those stitches were perfect, and you know it."

It was in response to the insult I'd dropped just before striding down this hall. An insult I'd given because we always picked at each other. However, it *wasn't* a warranted insult because the stitches he'd put into my teammate—*my* teammate! —were fucking perfect.

I was just upset because he'd put in those perfect stitches because *I* hadn't been there to help.

And yes, I got that it was a stupid reason to be upset.

It was just. The man. Was so. Freaking. Infuriating.

Luckily (though was it *really* lucky?), I was used to being infuriated by Linc. Since the moment I'd been recruited to KTS —going from M.D. to field medic to secret agent—he'd made it a point to piss me off.

First, as the man I'd shadowed to learn the ropes at KTS, thus dealing with no little amount of condescension and disdain.

Then as a fellow doctor (one with an equal rank, thank me very much) on the committee I worked on during my non-mission time. Our job was to write policies and procedures, to authorize, create, and vet new cutting-edge medical treatments. But the man questioned literally—*literally!*—my every decision. He pushed and prodded and was beyond frustrating, even though I respected his attention to detail.

But now, the man had gone too far.

Because he was treating my teammates.

Teammates who'd needed his treatment. Teammates whose lives he'd probably saved—which wasn't the point.

Nope.

The important point in the mental Olympics I was conducting was that the man was infuriating and annoying and . . . well, *infuriating*.

So. *There.*

Linc cleared his throat. "Am I *keeping* you?"

I smiled, knew it was sharp at the edges. "The stitches were perfect . . . ly adequate," I told him, shaking off his hand and moving back down the hall.

"Perfectly ad—" He broke off, and I heard his footsteps trailing me.

Do not engage.

Do *not* engage.

I didn't need to get drawn into yet another battle with this man.

Plus, if I hurried, I could make it to the airport in time to catch the plane back to England and be back, reviewing my policies and procedures, before the clock struck midnight.

Like some pathetic version of Cinderella.

Except instead of the pumpkin coach, I had my files.

Just as I preferred.

Ignoring the man dogging my steps, I pushed through the door that led into the underground garage and punched in my pin code on a panel hidden near the entrance. It slid open to reveal several sets of keys, each of which would work on the community cars that were parked here and available for KTS use.

This satellite base wasn't large, and it didn't have a built-in airstrip like the headquarters in England, but it wasn't missing many of the creature comforts we'd become used to as agents.

Bonus in this case, since the key fobs were interchangeable, I would drive to the airport, park the car, and keep the set with me.

Another agent would pick the car up later and use it when they flew in.

Like those scooter rentals littering the sidewalk.

Only these were much nicer—and fully bulletproof—cars.

Also, let it be noted that I was thinking about cars and scooters and interchangeable key fobs because I was desperately trying to *not* think about Linc—and the fact that he was behind me, trailing very close, his spicy scent teasing my nose, his heat at my spine.

Or maybe that was my imagination.

Because there was one additional reason this man drove me crazy.

I wanted him.

So. Fucking. Bad.

But . . . I'd given it a shot. I'd worked up my courage. I'd asked him to go on a date with me.

And . . . he'd turned me down.

Flatly. Coldly. Without hesitation.

God, it was *so* critically embarrassing. I'd been beyond excited to ask him. Yes, I'd had a couple of drinks, but we'd been working together a lot, and he'd thawed out, been more relaxed. Truthfully, we'd been having a lot of fun together, sharing a few late nights, discussing difficult cases, eating over our laptops, and I'd thought . . .

I'd thought he'd felt that connection, too.

Clearly, I'd been wrong.

Beyond wrong.

"No, Olive," he'd snapped when I'd invited him to dinner of the non-working variety. His gray eyes stormy and filled with frost, his lush mouth pressed flat, his tone cutting. "Not now. Not *ever*."

And so, I'd closed that door. Permanently. Thrown a dead bolt, squirted liquid nails around the frame, hammered in some metal ones, just for good measure.

Because I wasn't a glutton for punishment.

A man treated me like shit? Well, he wasn't ever getting another invitation from me, and I certainly wasn't going to *ever* treat him with a modicum of friendship. Respect? Yes. Professionalism? Certainly.

But friendship or more?

Abso-fucking-lutely not.

He was dead to me and would remain so for all of eternity.

So, here we were. Me pretending to be annoyed, snapping at him so I forgot to be hurt. Him furious and snapping back, those angry eyes locked on me during every interaction.

It was the perfect workplace situation.

I loved it.

Also, this just in, I loved sarcasm just as much.

"Olive—"

He grabbed my arm again.

I shook him off. Again. "Don't touch me," I hissed.

He lifted his palms in surrender, stepped back.

I forced myself to take a breath, to grab on to a modicum of kindness and graciousness, like my grandmother had taught me. At the very least, I could end this torture with that. "Thank you for your work on my teammates."

Gray eyes edged in storm clouds. That mouth not flat but rather plump and tempting. He stepped a little closer. "I don't do this for *thank yous*." A beat. "And I know you don't either."

I didn't. But that also didn't matter.

I shrugged, started to step away.

"I wanted to talk to you—"

Stopping, I met his eyes. "About what?"

Now, regret slipped into his expression. "About that night. I want you to know that I didn't mean to—"

Oh lord, now he was going to give me some excuse for why he didn't want to date me. How absolutely fucking pathetic. And miserable.

That, too.

"It's fine," I told him, lifting the key fob and striding toward the nearest car. "It's for the best anyway—"

"Olive, I wanted—"

"Obviously, it wouldn't have worked out. We're too different, and we work together, and—"

"It wasn't that I *didn't* want you—"

I clicked the button to unlock the car, unable to hear anything but my pulse pounding in my ears, my embarrassment making the *thrum-thrum* nearly deafening. "I get it, Linc," I told him. "Let's just forget it happened."

I yanked open the door.

And the world exploded.

CHAPTER TWO

KTS Satellite Base
Western Georgia
16:30hrs

Linc

I HEARD THE CLICK.

And was moving before my brain fully processed what that meant, grabbing Olive around the waist and yanking her away from the car, diving behind a large concrete pillar just as the explosion detonated.

That force sent me crashing into the support beam, and I shifted, pinning Olive beneath me just as a rush of heat blasted over us.

Loud.

That was all I could process at first, just the roar of the explosion, my ears screaming in protest, my eyes slamming shut against the bright light and the debris flying.

Something hit me hard in the back, hard enough to make all the air squeeze out of my lungs, pain radiating along my spine. But I couldn't focus on the hurt burning through me, not when, at the same time, Olive cried out beneath me—a sharp shriek of agony that had any discomfort of my own immediately disappearing.

I pushed off her, finding my feet, my gaze assessing the space, making sure it wasn't at risk of collapse.

The garage appeared mostly intact, a scorch mark on one wall, concrete chipped off in some places to reveal the rebar beneath, but for the most part unscathed. Impressive, especially considering the force of the blast we'd just experienced. On the other hand, the cars—bulletproof but not bomb-proof, a fact I made note of to have the technology section of KTS remedy as quickly as possible—were crumpled in on themselves and one another, twisted metal thrown in all directions.

"It looks safe enough," I said, "but we should—"

"Your back," Olive whispered.

A note in her voice had me turning back to face her, guilt ricocheting through my insides as I realized I should have assessed her for injuries first.

"*Fuck*."

I dropped to my knees, tearing off my shirt, ignoring the burst of pain the movement caused. I folded the material into a pad, quickly pressed it to the huge gash on her abdomen.

"Your back," she breathed. "Bleeding . . ."

Not nearly as much as she was.

"Ol—"

Her hands covered mine, taking over on the pad, somehow holding it in place even though her skin was beyond pale, her fingers trembling.

"Get help," she ordered.

Knowing there was nothing further I could do for her and understanding that the only way I could help her was to go get that help, I shot to my feet, running for the door into the facility.

It burst open before I could reach it, my teammates flooding out, guns in hand, body armor strapped on.

"Jack," I said to the first person who'd run through the door.

"Grab a stretcher." I reached inside, snagged the med pack that hung just inside the door, sprinting back to Olive, and dropping to my knees. I tore the kit open with no heed to sanitization or organization, tossing everything aside except for the one thing I needed.

The special bandage this woman and I had just trialed and approved.

I tore it open with my teeth, yanking away the T-shirt, then slapping the bandage over the wound, knowing it was the only thing that would work to stem the flow of blood until I could get her to the operating room.

"Radio down," I ordered Hannah, my team leader. "Tell them to prep OR 2."

Lily, another trained medic, dropped down next to me. "What do you need?"

I began rattling off orders.

Olive coughed, and I couldn't ignore the fact that it brought up blood. "Relax," she said, wiping the back of her hand over her lips, leaving her skin stained red. "It's just a little internal bleeding."

"Shut up," I snapped, knowing it would give her more fodder for her teasing about my lack of bedside manner, but the woman was bleeding out and making jokes.

For fuck's sake.

With a sharp tug—one that made her cry out and one that killed me inside—I secured the special bandage. It was an upgrade on our old clotting pack and would keep her stable until I could get her onto the operating table.

"Where the fuck is Jack?" I snapped.

"Here."

Lily jumped up and helped me prep the stretcher, and then with a quick flurry of movements, we got Olive onto it and were sprinting down the halls with her.

"Linc, put on a shirt," Olive ordered as we pushed into the room and lifted her onto the table. "Katie"—the nurse who was currently manning the infirmary—"get a line in my arm and push fifty mils of TXA . . ."

Her head flopped back, the arm she'd lifted in the direction of Katie flopping to the table as she lost unconsciousness.

I grabbed a scrub top, since that was the logical—and sanitary—thing to do, and yanked it on.

Katie glanced at me, already putting the line in.

"Make it a hundred mils," I told her, yanking on a clean pair of pants and shoes for good measure then stepping to the sink to scrub my hands and arms. My back was screaming, but it felt like the bleeding had stopped, so I knew that the injury there could wait.

Olive couldn't.

By the time my shoes were covered and my scrub cap tugged on, the line was in, fluids and the clotting drug KTS had developed were being pumped into her. Katie was monitoring her vitals, and another nurse had come in to assist. Mask and shield on, gloves on, and then I was stepping up to the unconscious body of the woman who'd both infuriated and made me near crazed with sexual desire in equal parts over the last years.

"Ready for a transfusion," I said to Lily, who had just completed her residency in order to be a more valuable asset to the squad.

"Blood type?" she asked.

I shouldn't know.

I didn't have a single reason *to* know.

Except . . . that I knew everything about this woman. Which is why I could say, "AB-positive."

No one questioned me knowing that. They *should* have—because how could I have possibly known that, especially for an agent who wasn't on my team. But thankfully, no one said a word. Lily just went to the phone, ordered up several bags of A-positive, since that was on hand and compatible with Olive's blood type, and then came back to my side and assisted me.

"Ready?" I asked, reaching for the corner of the bandage.

Lily nodded, grabbing some supplies. "Go."

I peeled back the bandage, and she packed the wound, slowing the bleeding as I worked to tie off the blood vessels, to find a permanent solution that would stop the flow. Clamping and cauterizing and suturing, focusing not on the woman and all my conflicted feelings, not on the people in the room with me, not on the blood flowing over my gloved hands and Lily continually replacing the packing, not on the transfusion being administered.

I was solely focused on the wound.

On finding every last source of bleeding.

On not stopping until I was able to save this woman's life.

Because I *had* to save this woman's life.

And then finally, everything was closed up, the bleeding was under control, and I was able to step back, to ask Lily to close the wound as I staggered to the next room and tore off my gloves, heart pounding, chest heaving, head hanging.

"She'll pull through," Lily said when she came in.

I wasn't so sure of that. Olive's vitals were shit, and the metal or whatever had sliced through her had practically razed her insides. It would be a fucking miracle if I hadn't missed tying off something, if she weren't bleeding internally even at this moment.

"There's nothing more we can do," she said. "And right now, I need to look at your back."

I turned to her, head pounding, vision swimming with exhaustion. "What's wrong with my back?"

"Burns, Linc," she said gently. "Your back is riddled with them."

"I'm fine." I took a step toward the door, rubbing my temple, the pounding transforming into a cacophony of noises and swirling vision.

I just needed to lie down for a bit, and I would be all right.

"No," Hannah said. "You're not. You look like you're going to pass out." She snagged my shoulder. "Infirmary. Now. And if

I need to make that an order from your commanding officer, I can do it."

"All right," I muttered. "I'll—"

I'd lifted my foot, readying to take a step toward the room down the hall . . .

But I didn't feel it touch the tile.

Because darkness swept up and sucked me under.

CHAPTER THREE

KTS Satellite Base
Western Georgia
09:47hrs

Olive

THE LIGHT WAS the first thing I processed, shining through my closed eyelids and making my brain thrum with pain.

But that pain quickly became negligible when compared to my stomach.

That felt like someone had taken a circular saw to it then jostled the blade through my insides, just for good measure. In fact, it hurt so much, overwhelmed my senses so rapidly that I found my breaths coming in short, staccato bursts.

Which did not feel great with a wound in my lower abdomen.

So, for long moments, I just lay there, trying to slow my breathing, to moderate my pain enough that I could open my eyes and get some freaking morphine.

"Easy now."

A gentle hand on mine, slightly calloused fingers brushing

my arm, shifting it and moving a cord along the inside before pressing a push button into my palm. "Morphine," Linc said. "It's ready for you."

I pressed the button. Once.

Even though I wanted to press it a dozen times, to waylay that motherfucker until the morphine filled my veins, until I drifted off into blissful abandon, I didn't. For one, morphine pumps didn't work that way—e.g. I couldn't overdose on this one—and two, part of me couldn't reveal my insecurities to this man.

I needed to be strong, to be tough.

To not be hurt.

Clearly not logical, I knew, because I unmistakably *was* hurt. So yes, it was illogical. But also, I couldn't be vulnerable with this man.

I just couldn't.

Luckily, the first pump of morphine took the edge off, allowed me to wait a few seconds before taking another. And by the time I pressed it a third time, I was floating blissfully on a cloud.

And floating enough to open my eyes.

God, he was pretty.

God . . . even doped up on morphine I wanted him.

God . . . that was pathetic.

"How's your back?" I asked, shifting my gaze from the chiseled planes of his jaw, the sharp lines of his nose, the stormy gray depths of his eyes.

Because he was looking at me gently.

And we couldn't have that.

Nope. No fucking way.

"Lily got the burns patched up." A shrug. "I'll be sleeping on my stomach for a while. I probably shouldn't say that, should I?" He lifted the sheet and my hospital gown, palpated gently around the bandage, peeling the corner up slightly to peek beneath at the stitches. All things I would do, which was why it took me a minute to realize he was basically staring at me naked.

No, of course, he wouldn't actually be thinking that.

If I'd learned anything about this man, it was that he was completely professional.

But . . . I was hurt and practically naked, and this man was looking at my body, a body I'd basically invited him to enjoy, a body he'd turned down with a sharp rebuke. So no, I wasn't feeling all that comfortable with him staring at me, no matter how professional.

"How's it feel?" he asked, smoothing my gown and the covers back down.

"I'll live," I said, resisting the urge to yank the blanket up to my chin. "You?"

His lips turned up. "I'll live." He made some notes in the computer, and I waited for him to leave as he slid in the keyboard tray, as he moved around the room, putting things back into place.

But he didn't.

Instead, he putzed about for a few minutes and then sat in the chair next to my bed.

Quietly.

Waiting . . . for something.

Fatigue was already creeping into the edges of my mind, threatening to take me back under. "What happened after I passed out?"

He shrugged. "We took you into surgery." A slight curve to his mouth, making a dimple appear in one cheek. "I followed your advice about the lines and TKA, though we had to double the dose."

"Of course, you did." I sniffed. "Why doesn't it surprise me that a *man* always has to make things bigger?"

Silence.

Then he roared with laughter, absolutely roared with it.

Meanwhile, I'd been serious. Which meant I did a fair amount of scowling at this man I was pretending not to want.

"I've always loved your sense of humor."

That was so not true. "Are you going to go away anytime this century?"

Warm, rough fingers covered mine, making me jump, causing pain to radiate down my side.

"Shit, sorry," he murmured, but he didn't let my hand go.

Just wove his fingers through mine and held tight.

"I'm tired," I whispered.

"Then sleep."

A shake of my head. "Not until you go."

His chuckle was rough, rumbling out of his chest, rubbing along my skin, combining with the fuzzy feeling in my head to make me shiver.

Then wince.

"You should take more morphine."

I shook my head again.

And . . . standoff.

"Why are you here?" I asked, my eyes struggling to stay open.

Calloused fingers running along mine. "Because I have a captive audience."

I frowned.

His fingers continued moving, lulling me into sleep, but I fought it. "What do you mean?"

"Hmm?"

"I asked—" A yawn punctuated my words.

"We almost lost you," he said. "You know that, right?"

Blinking at the change in topic, I focused on his face, on the concern in those dark gray irises, on the shadows beneath his eyes.

"You have a cut on your jaw."

A flash of that dimple. "Yes, Pops. I do."

More blinking. "What did you call me?"

He tilted his head to the side but didn't acknowledge my question, just said, "We had to give you a transfusion, and I lost count of the sutures."

"Probably because you were being stubborn about your back and shouldn't have been performing surgery." I lifted a brow, knowing I was being a bitch, but unable to stop myself. "Should I worry about surgical instruments being left behind?"

His laughter this time was quiet, a soft sound that rubbed against my skin like velvet. "No," he said. "Because Lily was there to keep me in line."

I snorted.

And still those fingers stroked—*up and down, up and down, up and*—

I yawned again.

"We almost lost you," he whispered.

"You already said that."

"It's something that's warranted to say twice."

"I don't know why you'd even care," I muttered.

"I care," he said, his voice going silky smooth. "I care because you're a good agent, a good friend, a good person." My lungs froze as he paused, my heart skittering in my chest. "I care because of what I was going to tell you earlier."

"*Before* the giant explosion?" I said dryly, needing to keep this light, to not process the words he'd just given me.

A chuckle. "Yes, before that."

"Pre-explosion. Got it." And saying that a second time made me realize I probably should have asked about it much sooner. There had been an explosion, likely an attack on the base, unless it had been some sort of freak accident, and I was thinking about Linc's dreamy eyes. I sighed, pushed that recrimination away. *Oh well.* I supposed I was allowed to be a little slow. I was recovering from major surgery, after all. "What's going on with that?" I asked him. "Did they find the source? Was anyone else hurt?"

His fingers stayed tangled with mine, but his other hand ran up and down my arm, sending a prickle of sensation through my nerves. It was somehow both perfect and also completely unpleasant.

"No one was hurt," he said, somehow seeming to sense that because he lifted his hands from my skin and sat back somewhat gingerly in his chair. "No source yet, but Laila and Ryker think it was a bomb meant for them."

My eyes widened, and I tried to sit up. *"What?* Are they okay?"

He was gentle as he coaxed me to lie back down. "They're fine. We were the only ones in the garage, so aside from the cars being totaled and some scorch marks in the concrete, the base is fine."

Well, that explained what had cut me.

It must have been a piece of metal from one of the vehicles. That was the only thing that could explain the clean lines of my injury. It certainly hadn't been an impact wound from the concrete.

"Is everyone else okay?"

"You asked that already," he said gently, smoothing back my hair. "Everyone is fine, but the entire base is on total lockdown. The teams are going through and searching every inch of the compound to make sure there are no other dangers, and anyone who isn't on that is rotating through patrols."

I nodded, but that information didn't answer the most important question.

"How could someone get in with a bomb?" I glanced up at him. "We're supposed to be completely secure. Someone would have to have credentials to—" I broke off, yawned again.

"Rest now," he ordered. "We'll figure out the answers to those very important questions later."

"Sarcasm doesn't work on you," I muttered.

A brush of his fingers on my cheek. "Not being sarcastic," he said.

Exhaustion was making my limbs heavy, my lids kept being

dragged down, forcing me to almost have to physically yank them open. "But what if—"

"Olive," he murmured. "Rest. We've got it for now."

His fingers stroked across my forehead, smoothed back my hair, and reflexively, my eyes shut, sleep inched closer. I fought the fatigue, struggled to stay above the fog, above slipping away.

But then he smoothed my hair again, murmured softly once more, "We've got it, sweetheart, I promise."

And I fell headlong into sleep.

———

HUMMING WOKE ME UP, and I blinked against the bright lights.

All I knew for certain was that it wasn't Linc.

Even as I'd lost and gained consciousness over the last who-knew-how-many days, I'd always known when he was checking in on me. Even hurting, even under the influence of morphine, I'd experienced the same instant body awareness I always did—my nerves all firing, goose bumps on my skin, heat coiling in my abdomen . . . and farther south.

Aside from all that sensation missing, the voice doing the humming was feminine.

See? I could use my kick-ass deductive reasoning skills. Go me.

Squinting and still blinking, it took a moment until I could see who was in my room. Ava. My kick-ass, formerly closed-down, and oftentimes frightening friend was staring out the window and humming.

Incongruous action with the woman I'd known before she'd fallen for my teammate, Dan, and opened her heart to love.

But certainly not incongruous with the woman I knew now.

And I was happy for her—even though I was forcing myself to not be a giant, jealous baby.

I wanted *that.*

I was still happy for her.

As she kept humming, I squinted again, though this time not because I needed my eyes to adjust but rather because I was trying to figure out the song. It sounded familiar, like something I'd heard on the radio a million times before—

"Sugar!" I screeched, making Ava freeze.

Not jump, because she was too good of an agent to react in such a way, going still rather than flailing when surprised, as we'd all been trained to do. She spun carefully, and I grimaced, somehow having forgotten the woman was on crutches.

Christ.

I'd almost made the woman with a twice-broken ankle fall off her crutches.

Go me, again.

She hobbled my way—still infinitely more graceful than me, even on those metal sticks—and sank into the chair at the bedside, studying my expression closely. "You had me worried there for a second, Ollie."

I couldn't have that, so my answer was light. "A girl tries to take *one* drive."

Ava chuckled. "You should have known better than to leave without the team."

"Meh." Gingerly, I waved a hand. "You don't want the third wheel around."

"You'd never be the third wheel," Ava said. "You know, we all feel so lucky to have you on the team."

"That's because we're the *best* team."

"Damn right, we are." She lightly fist-bumped me when I managed to lift my hand a little higher.

Progress.

"Plus," I said, making sure to keep my tone teasing so she knew I was joking, "I'm not even the third wheel. Technically, I'm the fifth."

I *was* joking.

Sort of.

No—I mean *yes*, I was joking. My team *was* the best, and that was because of the people on it. Laila and Ryker had both been leaders on separate teams before they'd gotten married, and when they had navigated their way to a permanent relationship, Ryker had given up his position as a commanding officer, coming over to Laila's team when an opening had come up.

True love, those two had.

But it made sense.

Being an agent with KTS was a full-time job, and having *two* agents in one relationship, both with separate teams, plus the added responsibility of leadership? Well, that would have made it nearly impossible for them to see each other.

KTS itself was an offshoot of several branches of several countries' military organizations. It was jointly funded and technically operated outside of all those countries' purview, though we had the necessary funding thanks to some very deep pockets.

Pockets that ensured KTS's mission was fulfilled.

Our job?

To save the world.

Our job in slightly less dramatic terms?

To track down the worst of the worst bad guys and to bring them in. We worked in human trafficking, in drug rings, in mafia cases. The tougher the villain, the more diligently KTS's teams worked to take them down.

And we were successful, for the most part.

But there always seemed to be another bad guy to take the place of those we shut down.

It was like fucking whack-a-mole, but for the worst of the worst.

Disheartening at times. Rewarding at others.

And still, something I would never, ever trade.

Each team at KTS focused on a different case, and though sometimes our jobs overlapped and we worked together, for the most part, we—meaning the field teams—were made up of small cells designed to infiltrate, reconnoiter, and take down.

Laila's—and by extension, *my*—team was currently focused on breaking up a trafficking ring based in southern Italy.

We had cracked some of the code, saved some of the people being sold.

But many more were still out there, and many more were still vulnerable to being exploited.

Plus, in our investigation of the ring, we'd discovered that KTS had been betrayed by a former agent named Daniel. Long thought dead, he'd been pulling some puppet strings, putting both KTS and many innocent people at risk. It was devastating knowing that one of our agents would do that, would do something so against the organization's tenets, but I had seen enough bad things to understand that . . . it wasn't unusual.

Shitty people did shitty things.

So now, our principal focus would be hunting Daniel down and making him pay for what he'd done.

And that last thought was why I couldn't ever be a doctor in the real world.

No, I didn't like to hurt people—even bad ones—but I sure as hell didn't mind tracking them down so they could meet their comeuppance, all the more so when it wasn't dished out by my hands.

On rare occasions, I'd heal them enough so they could meet their comeuppance a second time.

See?

Immoral and against a doctor's ethics to do no harm.

But I supposed that was why I was with KTS.

I didn't fit the normal doctor mold.

"You wouldn't be the third or fifth wheel," Ava said, drawing me out of my head, "or anything in between. You're Ollie, and you're the shit."

"Only because I bring the pizza," I said lightly.

A smile. "That, too."

Then she surprised me by grabbing my hand. Ava wasn't a touchy-feely person, not in any way, shape, or form, but this was another way that being with Dan had changed her. She didn't actively recoil from contact, sometimes—like in this case —initiated it herself. She'd certainly loosened up in other ways, too, and I didn't feel like she was actively trying to keep her distance any longer or that Laila and I had to drag her into anything that resembled a semblance of socialization.

I was thrilled that my friend—who had been through so freaking much—had been able to find someone who loved her for everything she was inside.

Because she was fucking great.

"What'll it be this time?" I asked. "Should we torture the boys and make them eat soggy Hawaiian?"

She reached for a plate that someone had left for me on the rolling tray, bringing it in front of me so I could see the contents. "I don't think you'll be eating pizza anytime soon," she said. "It'll be . . . let's see what we've got here. Lime Jell-O and toast. Yum."

I made a face.

Her laughter, so infrequent before Dan, made her teasing tolerable. Even though, "I hate lime Jell-O," I grumbled.

She laughed again. "Well, Ollie, I'm sorry to say, but it might be a bit before you can torture the boys with Hawaiian pizza."

My stink face didn't relax.

"I promise, though, the moment you can scarf down pizza, I will be all over helping you stick it to the boys."

"Promise?"

She pressed her hand to her heart. "I promise."

"What do you know about the bomb?" I asked, transitioning to more important topics.

"Only that Laila had the residue tested and it's GHS."

My mouth fell open. GHS was a special explosive made exclusively by KTS's engineering squad. It was lightweight, safe to transport, and a small amount could create huge explosions. "But how?"

Her face hardened. "It's got to be Daniel. He's the only one with working knowledge of this base, the only one who could have gotten back in. Fucking hell, I only wounded him." She cursed. "I can't believe I shanked that fucking shot."

That shot being taken on a twice-broken ankle with limited rounds, her boyfriend bleeding out, and at a distance of several hundred meters. No big deal. "There were a lot of factors in that situation," I reminded her. "And none of them under your control." I narrowed my eyes. "Even if you did do more damage to that ankle, missy."

"Not by choice, I promise you. Now"—she pushed to her feet, got her crutches under her arms—"I'm on the next watch of the security cameras, so I'm going to at least make myself somewhat useful."

"Put up that ankle," I called.

Pale brown eyes rolled. "I've already gotten the order from Linc *and* from Dan. I don't need it from you."

"That's a lie," I muttered. "*I* should be the only one you take orders from."

"Yeah, yeah. Laila said the same thing." She started puttering toward the door. "I get the picture. I've got a long list of people to answer to."

"Exactly. Oh, wait," I added before she got too far. "Can you wheel the computer over to me?"

She lifted a brow, her lips twitching. "Wanting to check the job Linc did on you?"

Maybe.

So what?

"Just bring it over, okay?"

Chuckling under her breath, Ava crutched over to the computer, pushed the wheeled unit up to my bedside. She even helpfully lowered it so my fingers could reach the keyboard. Then she shuffled out.

And with my head clear, my pain reasonable for the first time in—I glanced at the computer's calendar—three days, I typed in my authorization code and pulled up my chart.

And read, my heart thudding in my chest, as the realization of how close I'd come to dying hit home.

I'd been in the gray space; one false move could have pushed me either way.

But Linc had hauled me back.

My lungs went a little tight, fear trickling through me as I read the description of the injury, as my eyes trailed across the list of medications, took in how much blood I'd been given. No wonder I still felt so incredibly weak.

No wonder these last three days had been primarily filled with unconsciousness and morphine highs.

Damn. It had been *close*.

I clicked out of my chart, ignoring the prickle on my nape, knowing it was just an after-effect because of the close call. Pushing that notion to the side, I ignored the spike of guilt for what I was about to do next and opened another chart.

Linc's chart.

Was it an invasion of his privacy? Probably. No. *Yes*, it was. But he'd been hurt too, and I needed—

To be nosy?

Yes. That.

So, I let the guilt ride, gave into the nosiness, and I just . . . scrolled past anything that didn't involve the treatment for the explosion three days before.

Some morals, I had.

And great, now I sounded like Yoda.

But fictional, green characters aside or not, I read the list of his injuries—bruising contusions and several second-degree burns on his back, a deep cut that had required sutures—and I couldn't believe that the man had been coping with all of that *and* somehow performed an emergency surgery to save my life.

He shouldn't have been standing, let alone been able to

perform the precise kinds of procedures he'd done to stop the bleeding and ensure I survived.

Not to mention the fact that he'd done it with no complications, under pressure, and with a skeletal team of agents and nurses, who just happened to be nearby. All while injured.

Then if I added in how he'd managed to get me out of the way of the worst of the blast, and . . .

The man was practically a superhero.

Ugh.

Heat skating across my skin.

My thighs quivered.

Double ugh.

I turned before he spoke, my inner Linc-detector fully up and running, even if my body wasn't.

"Checking my work?"

I clicked out of the screen, shoved back the keyboard, and winced—because shoving really wasn't on my list of approved activities. "Would you expect anything less?" I asked.

A smile.

No, not *a* smile.

The smile. The killer smile that had my insides turning to jelly and that trickle of heat turning into a torrent. Which shouldn't even be freaking possible! I was recovering from abdominal surgery, so I shouldn't have any sort of sexual desire.

But I did.

Because this man was a flipping superhero.

A superhero whom I owed a thanks.

It was just . . . that freaking gratitude was sticking in my throat, tangled up with the last time I'd tried to extend an olive branch to this man.

Still, my grandmother had raised me to be polite—or at least to have *some* manners.

So, the thanks needed to happen.

Triple ugh.

"No," he murmured, flopping down into the chair with a

move that should have made him cry out in pain, based on the injuries listed in his chart. That he wasn't—

The pieces clicked in my mind.

"You have the new bandages."

A nod. "Figured I might as well be the first guinea pig."

Excited now, I tried to prop my elbows beneath me, wanting to see, but unlike the keyboard on the computer, I couldn't drag him closer or examine his back from a prone position like I had the screen. Instead, all I got was a burst of agony, a curse leaving my lips, and my elbows collapsing before I even managed more than an inch up from the mattress.

"Easy," he said, leaning closer and gently resting his hand on my shoulder.

I was breathing heavily, trying to keep the inhalations and exhalations small and controlled so as not to exacerbate my wound, and the man touching me was not helping. But I did manage to get my breaths to slow, the pain to recede, and my gaze back on his. "How are they working?" I asked when I knew my voice would be even.

"I'll show you."

I started to tilt my head to the side, my lips parting to ask him what he meant—

Then he whipped off his shirt.

Just whipped it off and . . . *oh my.*

I mean, I had imagined this man without his shirt on, had wondered what he'd look like naked, and I supposed he'd taken it off during the explosion, used it as a pad on my wound, but I hadn't been aware enough then, and I certainly hadn't pictured—

This.

And oh, but it was glorious. The slightest bit of hair on his chest—just enough to scream that he was all manly and delicious, but not so much as to make it resemble a carpet. *Blegh.* Instead, I wanted to stroke it, could imagine what it would feel like against my skin, brushing over my nipples, sliding along my torso, down farther until he positioned himself between my thighs—

Clenching my jaw, I tried to force myself to focus.

But how could I?

The man's pecs were grabbable, his stomach was flat and etched into six crisp squares, and his tattoo trailing up and over one shoulder . . . fuck, I wanted to lick it, to trace its many lines with my tongue.

And considering that his tat covered more than half his chest and most of one arm, that would require a lot of licking, a lot of tracing.

Oh, the trials a woman had to bear.

Before I could focus further on the yumminess that was his happy trail disappearing under the waistband of his jeans *and* making my mouth water for a whole other reason, he spun around and showed me his back.

His strong, muscled, tasty looking back.

Yup. I had problems.

Control, Olive. Find some fucking control.

Right. I'd worked with this man for a long time and had never had difficulty with my control. Further that, I worked with sexy, built men *all* the time. Six-packs were like the currency at KTS, along with yummy arms, cut backs, and powerful thighs. Hell, I'd even seen more than my fair share of penises—which was maybe my least favorite body part to ogle, but my most favorite to feel.

Heh.

Except, it wasn't exactly funny, how much this man made me feel.

Why was it that Linc's respective parts somehow made my body stand up and take notice, when the rest of the male populace seemed to make me go just . . . *meh?* It was silly, and it wasn't helpful, and—

It wasn't pertinent to this conversation.

Well, not to the mental argument in my head, anyway.

Which thankfully was taking place *in* my head and not out of it because otherwise . . . critical embarrassment.

Kind of like the mortification staining my cheeks pink when he glanced over his shoulder and caught me staring. "How's it look?"

Damned fucking good.

But *that* wasn't the point.

I had worked with the engineering department to create these bandages, which basically took our clotting packs and jacked up their effectiveness significantly. They were packed with materials that could stop a significant amount of bleeding and was only activated by red blood cells. They also had another KTS-developed substance on them that promoted healing and reduced pain. One final compound was activated with spit—not the most sanitary, certainly, but desperate times in the field called for desperate measures. Anyway, a small amount of saliva hardened the bandage so it could be used as a splint or even to make a cast. That one-two-three chemical configuration had been my idea. If one of us got hurt in the field, time was critical and being able to use one dressing for multiple reasons—wounds, burns, broken bones—made my ability to treat agents much more efficient and effective.

The only difficulty had been adhesion.

"Are they staying in place?" I asked.

He nodded. "With the new pattern of glue on the wings, they've stayed in position. And the pain-relief has been incredible. I swear, I don't even feel like I was hurt." He reached into his pocket then held up his hand, showed me that he'd brought along one large enough to cover my wound. "Wanna try one?"

Even if it wasn't going to get me out of this hospital bed that much sooner, I would have jumped at the opportunity to try out this new tech. This was my baby, the thing I'd been working on for months. I needed. I wanted.

"Yes," I said, grabbing the corner of the blanket and lifting it off.

Linc set the bandage on the bed, shrugged back into his shirt, then moved to the door, snagging a pair of gloves from a box mounted near the frame. A moment later, he was back at my side, grasping the edge of my hospital gown and shifting it to reveal the standard-issue KTS bandage beneath.

Notice how I didn't make any allusions to him undressing me.

Nope.

That wouldn't be good.

This was strictly doctor and patient, no matter how good his hands felt on me.

Gah!

His hands didn't feel good. Nope. They were just hands administering treatment and that was it. *It!*

Then they actually *were* just hands administering treatment.

Because *shit* that didn't feel good on my stitches, being tugged this way and that as he peeled back the dressing.

"Sorry," he murmured, carefully easing the tape away from my skin. "I haven't actually had to change this while you were conscious, yet."

Which insinuated that he'd done it while I was unconscious.

And didn't that give me something to ponder.

Cute.

As in, had he thought I was cute while I was unconscious? Or as in, was that sarcasm because I was trying to deflect the thoughts away from something that made me uncomfortable? I hoped for the second. I feared it might be the first.

"Blegh," I muttered.

His gaze shifted, coming up to meet mine. "Blegh, what?"

I shook my head. "It doesn't matter."

Gray eyes on mine, studying me closely. "Hmm," he murmured, then focused back on the bandage.

"I didn't thank you."

He looked up again, and I was momentarily stunned by my blurt, so words didn't immediately come, making me unable to add anything more, except for a shrug. "We don't do this job for the thanks. You know that." The ghost of a smile. "I believe that's part of what we were arguing about before the explosion." He set the old bandage to the side, began to unwrap the new one. "The other thing—"

I grabbed his wrist. "Linc."

He froze, stared into my eyes, arm shifting so his palm was suddenly pressed to mine, fingertips tracing patterns gently on the surface. Then he lifted my hand to his lips, kissed my palm. "What, baby?"

More of me being stunned, only by the endearment this time.

Before I was over that, he was smoothing my hand down, returning to the bandage.

"What are you doing?" I whispered.

And I wasn't talking about treating my wound. I was talking about the fingertip stroking, the calling me baby, the kiss to my palm.

His eyes didn't come to mine this time, rather they stayed on my abdomen as he unwrapped the outer layer, as he carefully covered my wound. "I'm taking care of you," he said.

"I—" My mouth opened and closed. "I don't need you to."

Now his eyes came to mine. "I know." A beat. "But I'm doing it anyway."

CHAPTER FOUR

KTS Satellite Base
Western Georgia
17:47hrs

Linc

SURPRISE in those blue eyes of hers.

A bright cerulean I'd seen so often in the sky overhead that I'd figured it was the universe laughing at me.

A blue I'd never seen in another person—streaked with gold and gray, the clouds and the sun all coming out to play on a warm summer day. And that was what she'd brought.

I just hadn't been ready for it.

For a long time, I *couldn't* have been ready for that warmth.

But . . . times changed.

And I was hoping it wasn't too late. I'd bungled things badly, been a total asshat, and now I needed to show her that I wasn't normally like that—okay, so the last wasn't true. I could definitely be an asshat, and I'd demonstrated that quite clearly. The only difference was that I normally wasn't such a giant asshat to people like Olive.

People who were nice and smart and funny.

It was just . . . she'd made me feel too much on a day when I'd already been feeling too much, and then guilt had collided with the other strong emotions—with need and desire and respect and affection—to twist into a giant tangled ball that had made me lash out unforgivingly.

"What do you mean, you're going to do it anyway?" Her dark brown brows drew down.

"I mean, I'm going to take care of you."

I smoothed one side of the bandage.

"Okaaay," she said. "So once again, we're circling back to why in the ever-loving fuck you think I'd want *you* to take care of me. And further that, why you would think you had any right to—"

"I don't." I shrugged. "But I'm still going to do it anyway."

Her mouth fell open; a flush appeared on her cheeks.

God, she was pretty.

I finished with the bandage, tugged her gown back in place, the blanket up, then disposed of the dirty gloves and wrapping. But instead of leaving like she probably wanted me to, I made myself comfortable back in the chair at her bedside.

Her head tilted in my direction, eyes sparking in annoyance.

"Is there a reason you're still here?" she grumbled.

I nodded, rested my laced fingers on my chest. "I'm going to tell you a story."

For the second time in as many minutes, her jaw dropped open. "You cannot be serious."

"Oh, but I *can*," I said lightly.

Her brows drew together, then she narrowed her eyes at me. "You know what? I think this bandage is doing the trick." She propped her elbows beneath her. "I'm going to discharge myself." She reached for the computer.

Infernal woman.

Still, I wasn't going to engage in the discharging nonsense. She wouldn't have the strength to get out of bed, no matter how tough she was or how good the bandage was. But, as I'd learned over the years of dealing with her, I knew that arguing would get me absolutely nowhere.

So, I went for distraction instead.

"Did you know that we named it The Ollie?"

She froze in the six inches she managed to lift herself. "What?"

"The bandage. The engineering team and I agreed it should be named after you."

Her mouth opened and closed a few times, confusion in those blue depths. Confusion that enabled me to coax her back onto the mattress.

"It seemed only logical." I tucked the blanket around her again. Snugly. So it would be harder for her to escape.

"But I was hardly the only one to work on it."

I took the opportunity to smooth back her hair and fuck if it didn't feel like silk, even after these days in the hospital. Speaking of which, most people were a little rank after an extended stay, especially those in her position, in and out of consciousness, deodorant and sponge baths far down the list of priorities. But Olive smelled like heaven—roses and vanilla with a dash of spice—and I didn't miss the connection to the woman herself.

Sweet and feminine, but with thorns and a little attitude.

The absolute fucking perfect combination.

I wasn't the type of man who wanted all of one side or the other. I appreciated the fact that she could be a total badass, that she could take down an enemy, whether three hundred yards away or three *feet* away. But I also loved that she'd managed to hold onto more than a sliver of softness.

She cared about the agents, about the people they saved.

And not just in a sense that some of the agents did—that caring only due to the fact that saving them meant a successful mission. She cared well beyond that. Arranging for housing, making sure the kids got into good schools (even if she had to fund scholarships for them herself so they could afford tuition). Hell, I'd caught her baking a birthday cake for an eight-year-old who had been rescued from a trafficking ring not long before, simply because the little girl was alone and "deserved to have one happy memory." She'd not only gotten candles and sprinkles from somewhere, but she coaxed a dozen agents to sing Happy Birthday.

And she had produced a present—and not just a wrapped one. Because the next day, Olive had managed to track down the little girl's parents.

That had been a good day.

A happy ending, when all too often happy endings for those caught up in those rings didn't happen.

But that time we had managed to rescue the little girl before she'd been sold, and we'd found her family. She would probably always carry scars from her experience, but I was critically aware of both how resilient kids were and how easily these situations could go wrong.

That little girl, she was the one they all remembered when shit got dark.

Because of Olive.

Because she cared for those she saved, and those who did the saving.

But . . . who cared for her?

No one from what I could see. She was too busy giving herself to others to take care of herself, to make sure she had what she needed. So, since she was doing a shit job of it, *I* was going to care for her. *I* was going to make sure she had what she needed.

"You were the driving force of the idea," I said, interrupting her as she continued sputtering about it being a "team effort" and "many minds had worked on it."

"Linc, I still—"

"It's named The Ollie," I said. "It's already gone into production. End of story." I lifted my brows, waited for her to argue further, and based on the mutinous expression dancing across her face, additional arguments *would* be coming my way. Maybe just not right at that moment.

"I still think that the team should be included in the name somehow," she muttered.

"Great," I told her.

She brightened. "So, we'll work on a new name?"

I didn't hesitate. "Nope."

She sighed. "God, you're infuriating."

"No," I said. "What I *am* is going to tell you a story."

"You said that already," she grumbled. "And alas, no story is forthcoming."

"If you'd just stop interrupting me and actually let a man—"

She huffed.

I grinned.

"You just live to annoy the shit out of me, don't you?" More muttering.

Leaning forward, I stroked a finger down her cheek. "I do love the way your eyes flash when you're annoyed," I admitted. "But no, I do really need to tell you something. Will you let me?"

A muscle in her jaw twitched. "Will you promise to leave me alone after you do?"

"Yes."

She crossed her arms, winced, then uncrossed them. "Fine. Tell your magical story so you can get out of my hair already."

I tilted my head to the side, studied her totally kissable lips, those gorgeous blue eyes. "How did we go from you giving me your undying thanks for saving your life to you kicking my ass out the door?"

"Easy," she told me. "Because you're annoying."

My grin slipped free. "And I'll continue being so as long as it makes your eyes shoot sparks like that," I said. "They're so fucking pretty when they do that."

She inhaled sharply.

And cursed, bringing a hand to her side.

"Sorry," I murmured.

"Why do you keep saying these things?" she asked, her brows furrowed again, a tiny V in between them that called to my lips, made it almost impossible to not kiss that little furrow away. "You don't want me." She shook her head. "You made that quite clear."

"Oh no," I said. "I've wanted you from the moment you strode onto the base, stuck your hand out, and introduced yourself." I circled her wrist with thumb and forefinger, running the former over the soft skin on the inside. "Do you know that I can remember what you were wearing?"

Her lips parted. Just slightly, a quiet breath sneaking out from in between them. "What are you saying? I—" She swallowed. "I don't understand. I mean, I asked you out, and you said—"

I squeezed lightly when her words faltered. "It has to do with the story I need to tell you."

Blue, *blue* eyes studying mine, and I could have sworn the ice that had been present in those depths since the moment I'd well and truly fucked up, melted slightly, and for a moment, I had hope that I'd be able to smooth things over.

Then the ice reappeared.

And I had the thought that my hope was about as good as a spoon when my enemies had AK-47s. I could do some damage, take down a few of them, but in the end, it was more than likely I would succumb to their stronger firepower. More than likely, my story wouldn't make one bit of difference.

I needed to tell her, anyway.

"So, get on with this tale of yours, already," she snapped, yanking her hand out of my grip, bringing it up to her forehead, and I saw that her fingers were shaking; her skin had gone pale.

I was hurting her.

Again.

When she was recovering from almost dying.

"It's okay," I said, preparing to stand. "I'll come back and tell you another time."

"No." She snagged my hand. "Wait," she said, tugging it slightly. Her fingers still trembled, and the force with which she held me in place was one I could have easily broken. But I *couldn't* leave. Not when she'd reached for me, not with her hand wrapped around mine. "I'm sorry," she said.

I brought my free hand on top of both of ours. "It's—"

"Not okay," she interrupted. Her fingers convulsed in mine. "The truth is that my pride was hurt, and I'm taking it out on you." Pink flared across her cheeks. "You were right to turn me down. It would have only complicated things."

It was my turn to say, "No," and I nearly gasped when her eyes came to mine again. They were swirling with emotion, pinning me in place, making me forget what it was to breathe, to exist in anything outside those primal, bright blue eyes. "I should have explained myself better then. I was a total jackass and—" I pulled away, thrust a hand through my hair. "And I'm the one who owes you an apology. This could have all been different if only I'd—"

I broke off, words failing me.

Until she reached for my hand again. "Stories usually start with *Once upon a time,*" she said, her tone light and teasing and so much like *Olive* that my heart actually squeezed.

Then the sass came back.

In the form of her free hand making a circular, "Come on" motion, her lips curved into a smirk. "And then what happened?" she asked, the snark fully present.

Sweet.

Spicy.

My kryptonite.

Which is probably why I managed to blow it even further.

"I'm married," I said.

CHAPTER FIVE

Olive

"Um, excuse me?" I asked, completely aware that my mouth was flapping open and closed like a fish, that I must certainly appear to be completely befuddled.

Because . . . *um* . . . what the *fuck?*

Linc slipped his hand from mine, effortlessly breaking my hold that had been weakened by both the injury and the complete and utter shock that his pronouncement had produced.

He paced away, stopped with his back to me, and I watched both hands come up to grip his hair. I'd seen him make that gesture enough times to know that when he turned around, the strands would be mussed, twin tracks on either side of his head, one lock drifting forward to curl over his forehead.

Normally, I'd be fighting the itch to smooth it back.

Today, I was fighting the urge not to smack him.

He was *married?* Why in the fuck hadn't he just said so? What was so complicated about that?

Just tell me he had a wife, and then I would have certainly backed off.

And, also, what the fuck?

He was in my hospital room, tracing little patterns on my skin, calling me baby, and smoothing back my hair and—

He. Was. Married.

What in the fuck-all was wrong with this man?

"It's not what you think."

I forced my eyes away from his. "*I'm married* seems pretty crystal clear."

"Ollie—"

"That's Olive to you," I muttered. "Or perhaps, Dr. Jacobs would be better."

"Ollie," he said again, and I had to bite back my retort. I couldn't physically force him from this room, so the easiest thing was to let him say his piece, and then I could go back to pretending the man was dead to me.

I kept my eyes on the computer, ground out. "Once upon a time . . ."

A sigh. "Won't you look at me?"

"Story," was my only response.

Silence.

Then he shifted, taking the seat next to my bed again, and saying, "Once upon a time, there was a man desperately in love with his wife. This man loved her beyond reason, and even though he was away for long periods and couldn't tell her anything about his job, he still was desperate to make things work with her." A short breath. "And for a while, they did make things work, and things were good."

My heart had picked up the pace about halfway through that first sentence, and it continued to speed as he spoke, thrumming in my veins and making it difficult to concentrate on what Linc was saying.

"But then this man came home early from a mission one day to find that his wife didn't love him the same way. In fact, she was in love with the real estate agent who'd recently sold the couple their very first house." He cleared his throat. "Things imploded. Stuff went to hell. And . . . when he was at his lowest point, having just signed the papers to turn over that house to his wife and the realtor, a beautiful woman asked him on a date."

My head turned; my eyes collided with his.

"And this man was so fucked up inside that he lashed out at this wonderful, smart woman, who didn't deserve to be treated that way."

Eyes stinging, I reached for him. "Linc."

"So, this man—" He shook his head. "No. Not this man. Me. *I'm* sorry. I was an asshole, and my reaction was totally uncalled for." A beat. "*That's* what I was trying to tell you in the garage," he whispered. "Before the fucking world exploded. That I'm so, so sorry, and I—"

"Hey," I said. "It's all right."

"It's not—"

Through some Herculean effort, I managed to place a finger over his lips. "It *is* all right," I said, fixing him in place with a stare.

He peeled my finger back, pressed a kiss to my palm. "Thank you," he murmured. "And for the record, I am still married, but not for much longer. I'm just waiting on the final paperwork to make the divorce official. I wouldn't—" He shook his head. "With you—I wouldn't do—"

"I know," I said.

And it was true.

Somewhere deep inside of me, I did know that. I *had* known that, even if it was safer for my heart to pretend I hadn't. Because even though he'd hurt me, I'd always known he was a good man. He was a good agent, a good doctor, and . . . I liked him.

His eyes skated away. "I just wanted you to know." He cleared his throat. "I thought you *needed* to know."

"Thank you," I murmured.

Quiet stretched, and it wasn't comfortable in the least.

Then he placed his hands on his thighs. "I should go." A forced smile. "I did promise, after all." He moved toward the door.

His name bubbled out of my throat. "Linc."

He stopped, rotated back to face me.

"Or," I whispered. "You could stay. The Gold are playing tonight, and Brit is in net."

His mouth dropped open. "Really?" he asked, and I knew he wasn't talking about the fact that the Gold were playing their starting goalie.

I smiled. "On one condition."

"Name it."

"I'd really love to eat something that isn't Jell-O."

He laughed, came close, and brushed a finger down my cheek. "I think I can arrange that."

———

"DAMN." He winced.

And it wasn't from his injuries.

Rather it was from the hit that Dan's sister had just taken behind the net.

Yup, that was correct. My teammate's sister was the first woman to play hockey in the NHL. She was the starting goalie for the team and had led them to two Cups (with plenty of help from her talented offense and defense) over the course of her career. I'd met her several times while on assignment with Dan in San Francisco or the occasional road trip when our travel schedules had aligned. Hell, I hadn't even been a hockey fan before I met her. Then she'd given us tickets to a game . . . and the atmosphere of the Gold Mine—their home arena—had just been incredible.

The roar of the crowd vibrating through my stomach. The speed of the game, the hits, the passes, the goals. I'd been hooked, so now I followed the team as much as I could.

This was early in the season, so the stakes weren't high like during a playoff run.

But it still gave me the chills when I watched them skate.

Hell, if I didn't have such a hard-on for the man sitting next to me, I might have tried to convince Brit to set me up with one of her teammates.

Hockey butts = chef's kiss.

But the fact of the matter was that I *was* hung up on Linc, on the steady, quiet presence he brought to the room, the easy confidence with which he carried himself. He knew he was smart, knew he was attractive, and despite us crossing swords at regular intervals, he wasn't arrogant.

Just comfortable in his own skin. A fact that made him very appealing.

Something that made him all the more likable?

That confidence wasn't all-powerful.

He'd been hurt by his ex, and God, I had plenty of experience having my heart broken. Especially in the medical field, and even more so in this field.

We were away more often than we were home.

We were in dangerous situations, sometimes injured, and we never could talk about it to civilians.

Which was the other reason I'd never asked Dan's sister to hook a girl up.

I couldn't date someone from the real world.

It was destined to implode.

As what had unfortunately happened for Linc.

Who was wincing right along with me at the hit. Well, it was less intentional check and more freaking *yard sale* in front of Brit's net. Two skaters had gotten tangled, and they'd slid into the goal, knocking her down, sending equipment flying, and playing clown car in between the posts.

How many skaters could fit inside?

Well, *three* appeared to be the limit.

I breathed a sigh of relief when I saw Brit push past the scuffle in front of the goal and skate to the bench. The rest of the guys were pushing and shoving, and I always had a chuckle when she casually left them to it and went to get some water.

Carry on, boys, she seemed to be saying. *I'll be over here to get on with it when you're done.*

"Good thing she's got all that padding on," he muttered. "That looked hard enough to take down a locomotive."

I smiled. "Have you not watched a lot of hockey?"

He shook his head. "Nope. More of a basketball fan, myself."

"Sacrilege! Hockey has it all. How can you possibly—?"

"Are you going to eat the dinner I so painstakingly retrieved for you?"

"You mean the one you walked to the phone in the corner of the room and ordered up for us? The same one that was delivered right to my beside?"

His mouth quirked. "Yup. It was really quite difficult."

I rolled my eyes.

"So?"

My brows lifted.

"You going to eat?"

No, I wasn't. Or at least not any more than I already had. The internal damage from my injury hadn't affected any of my organs—somehow—but I still wasn't up to eating a full meal, even with my special bandage.

I'd managed a bit of pasta, some salad, to drink a glass of hot tea.

But my body had told me that was enough for now.

Later, I might try again.

Or I might even be forced to stick with that freaking lime Jell-O.

"I'm full," I said, pushing the tray away when he nudged it a little closer.

He rolled it back. "You hardly ate enough to feed a bird. Try a little more. That's the only way you're going to get strong enough to get your ass out of this bed."

"I will," I said, pressing it away again. "Later."

Linc's eyes flashed, lightning mixing with stormy gray. "No." He pushed it in. "Now."

I fixed him with a look, clenched my teeth together, and inhaled sharply through my nose. "I'm full now. I'll eat more in *a little while.*"

"No," he repeated, shoving it even closer. "You'll try *now.*"

"Are you fucking serious?" I exploded. "Are you seriously trying to force-feed me?"

"No," he gritted. "I'm trying to make sure the woman I saved from dying three days ago gains her strength back, so she can go back to being the kickass agent I know she can be. Is that too much to ask?" He tossed up his hands. "God save me from stubborn women."

Okay, there was a little bit there in the middle that was kind of sweet.

The rest of it was . . . infuriating.

As I was struggling to hold onto the sweet part and to not turn the whole fucking tray over on his head—even though I was weak, I knew I could find the strength to at least manage that much—he picked up the fork, scooped a bite of pasta up on the tines, and shoved it through my still-forming-a-rebuke lips.

Sputtering, I managed to chew and swallow without spitting it out on the blankets.

"See?" he said. "You can eat more." He lifted the fork again.

I grabbed his hand, digging my fingers into a pressure point between his thumb and pointer finger, and digging hard, because the stubborn fuck . . . kept . . . coming. Finally, his hand spasmed, the fork fell to the blankets, and I ended up with pasta on my bed, despite my earlier efforts to prevent that exact thing from happening.

"Don't you fucking dare," I growled when he went to reach for it with the other hand. I snatched the fork up and tossed it on the plate, shoving the tray back hard enough that it nearly toppled over. Then I turned to glare at him. "You are *way* out of line."

His eyes narrowed and in the next heartbeat, his hand was free, speeding toward my face fast enough that I started to flinch.

But before my body could complete the movement, his palm was gently cupping my cheek, stroking over my skin, brushing along my jaw, flicking up to trace behind my ear. "You need to eat."

His touch almost made me forget myself. My fury.

The man was a fucking wizard.

Luckily, it was *almost* because I was a fucking KTS agent, and it would take more than some magical fingertips to get me to cave—though not much more because . . . *magical fingertips*.

Still, I managed to retain some semblance of my dignity and smacked his hand away.

"I'm nauseous and full. Do you want me to puke on you?" I snapped, glaring at the red stain on my blanket. To get a new one, I'd have to ring the nurse, so I'd just have to deal with it for now. But I knew the mark and the *ode du garlic* would annoy me until I got a fresh set.

"No," he said, standing up, and I sent up a prayer to the universe for the man finally leaving. I'd be free of this infernal man, and then I could focus my attention on recovering and figuring out how to track Daniel down.

Because he'd come for my people.

And he needed to pay.

I suspected I was even furious enough since he'd dared attack Dan and Ava that I might be able to dish out that punishment myself. I also suspected I wouldn't get the chance, because my retribution would be far down the list.

That was fine.

I'd just help with the planning, and maybe I could get a kick or two in when he was down.

I'd be good at it—the kicking *and* the planning. But most especially the latter, because I was doing a lot of plotting of late, starting with planning how easily I might be able to stick that fork into Linc's perfect ass.

He wouldn't be permanently injured.

Just four little prick marks to remind him to not be . . . well, an *ass*.

Instead of bringing the tray over like I half-expected, he moved to the door, opening and shutting it behind him. Without another word.

And he didn't come back.

A curl of disappointment wove through me, even though I told myself that I would need to turn in my feminist card if I was really feeling upset about him leaving after the stunt he'd just pulled.

But apparently . . . I'd need to turn it in.

Because the food thing aside—I truly *was* going to puke on the next person who tried to force me to choke down something else—there was nothing I loved more than fighting with Linc.

He was infuriating.

He could piss me off faster than any other person on the planet—or at least any of them that I'd met.

But . . . I liked the man.

Sighing, I shifted the blanket so the stain wasn't so obvious then settled back in to watch the game. It was fine. Same as I didn't want the food, I didn't want to spend time with Linc anyway. He could take his alpha, broody ass right out that door and never come back.

Good riddance.

Too bad I couldn't even sound like I believed the words, even in my own head.

"Hockey," I whispered. "Hockey." I focused on the screen, watching as Blue, one of the Gold's star forwards, was carrying the puck up the ice, streaking toward the net and—

I gasped when the blanket was torn off me.

The crowd cheered distantly in the background, the goal song playing through the TV, but I barely heard it.

Because Linc was back, had returned on silent freaking feet and was smoothing a fresh blanket over me. I saw that it was one of the new ones we'd just started using—slightly weighted at the edges to provide better rest for patients like me who enjoyed multi-night stays—instead of the old and slightly frayed version I'd been using before. And I knew it was silly, but part of me *aw*-ed inside when I noticed that detail, saw that he'd tracked it down instead of just grabbing one of the older ones.

Yes, I was fully aware that I was losing it.

Furious at him for feeding me.

"Awing" at a flipping blanket.

He finished tucking it around me, sat down, and diverted his eyes to the screen, not saying a word as he focused on the game.

For my part, I didn't say anything, either.

But I did cuddle up beneath the blanket with a satisfied smile.

CHAPTER SIX

Linc

I SET down the file with a sigh, knowing that I needed to focus on the words on the printout but unable to.

I'd sat with Olive until late the night before, watching the hockey game.

At first, in long, semi-uncomfortable silence.

Then in tentative conversation.

She'd asked me about my team's mission—we were focused on taking down a ring of criminals who were smuggling opioids into rural communities all across the Midwest, and it was a tricky quagmire to navigate. We'd had some success of late, interrupting a large shipment, but the group had ties to the Russian mob, to the Mikhailova clan that her team had been focusing on taking down over the last few years.

They'd been partially successful, too, removing several top members from the picture.

The difficultly was that the Russians had teamed up with an Italian crime group, and that made them twice as hard to pin down.

Ava had been seriously injured during their last mission, and again while here in Georgia on a short vacation when Daniel—not to be confused with her boyfriend, Dan, Brit's brother and not a fucking turncoat—had cornered them at Dan's farm and tried to take them out. Lucky for both of them, Ava was lethal, even with a broken ankle, and Dan was strong as a fucking bull to be able to power through getting shot.

It was those injuries I'd been treating—recasting the broken ankle, stitching up the thankfully through-and-through bullet wound, when Olive had flown in, we'd had words and then been caught in the explosion.

Shoving the file away from me in disgust, I stood up, knowing she would probably be uninjured right now if we hadn't had such an antagonistic relationship. She would have stayed in England, wouldn't have been caught in the collateral that was Daniel's mess.

Well, *KTS's* mess.

Because they already had to deal with the Italian mafia, the Russian mob, drug dealers based in Asia, Europe, and Central and South America, and now they also had to devote resources to taking down a former agent who was a formidable foe. Daniel knew KTS, knew how they operated, and that put them all at risk.

But—and the reason for his frustration with that fucking file on his desk—there was no proof that Daniel had been here at all.

No sign on the cameras—and their security system was the most comprehensive that could be implemented. It couldn't be hacked, and even if it had been, there were multiple layers of backups upon backups. Further that, there had been no odd logins, iris scans, or card swipes at the readers on any entrance or exit. Lest anyone think they could fake those, full iris scans were required to get into any part of the building, including the garage, and there were keypads embedded into the concrete walls requiring logins. Those keypads were scattered through the area and could only be accessed via codes on a fob that agents wore around their necks. The fob's codes changed every sixty seconds and only worked to authorize those codes and to generate new ones if it was in contact with the agent's DNA *and* a special implant that had been adjusted to be unique for each KTS member. The latter had been implemented after Daniel had left.

Hence, more things that were concerning.

But beyond that advanced bit of technology, we had card readers on every door leading in and out of specific areas (e.g. engineering, the lab, sleeping quarters, the infirmary, the cafeteria, the library). Those were placed strategically to be able to easily track movements for scenarios just like this one. But we hadn't gotten a ping from Daniel's old card on the readers, and no blips on the cameras, no sightings from those working the front gate. The regular patrols had similarly not seen anything.

There was nothing there.

Nothing on our security measures.

It was like a fucking ghost had deposited that bomb.

Or . . . there was another traitor in KTS.

One who was working with Daniel.

One who had a personal bone to pick with Daniel's former teammates Laila and Ryker, and had been convinced to carry out Daniel's revenge.

Because no one suspected that Olive could have been the real target.

She didn't have the ties, the past connections to be in the crosshairs. She was simply too new and too inexperienced in the field to have been the intended victim. That wasn't to say she wasn't a talented agent. Just that almost anyone else on her team would have made a better target.

But she was the one who'd nearly died.

Sighing, I shoved my hair back out of my face, made a mental note to get a freaking haircut, and then stalked off down the hall. I wanted to be alone. I wanted to beat someone up, to use my fists to slake this frustration, but since I couldn't do the latter, I would take advantage of the late hour and nearly empty corridors and go shoot some shit at the range.

The infirmary wasn't far from the office I used when on shift at this base, though my team and I tended to be stationed at the main headquarters in England when not working on this drug ring.

Still, it was convenient to have space to work in multiple locations.

It was also frustrating when neither of those locations ended up being helpful in any fucking way.

Still, there were plenty of guns, plenty of ammunition, and since I couldn't shoot anyone at the moment, I'd take out my frustration on a paper target.

Good times.

Except just as I was getting ready to swipe my card on the reader that was by the exit to the infirmary, I saw a flash of movement out of the corner of my eye.

No. Not a flash.

A slow-moving gait.

I spun and promptly lost my temper. "What in the fuck do you think you're doing?"

Olive froze, guilty expression on her face, even as she tried to melt back into the shadows.

I lifted a brow.

She stopped moving.

Or at least, she stopped trying to hide in the shadows. Instead, she took a step toward me, straightened her shoulders, and lifted her chin. "I couldn't sleep," she announced by way of explanation. "So, I'm going for a walk."

My eyes drifted down, taking in her stocking feet, the soft gray sweats, the loose T-shirt.

She huffed, lifted one foot to show me the bottom. "They're lined with non-skid tread," she muttered. "Relax."

I lifted my other brow.

"I was cold, all right? And I'm not stupid enough to have worn regular ones and slipped." Another mutter, this one accompanied by her crossing her arms.

"I didn't say you were."

"You implied it"—she waved a hand in his direction—"with those fucking eyebrows and all their judginess. Put the scowl away and just . . . go suck a lemon for fuck's sake!"

I froze, went ramrod still.

Then I burst into laughter.

Because seriously, "Go suck a lemon?"

"Ugh!" she snapped, shoving past me.

Or started to, anyway, because the moment she reached my shoulder, she'd wobbled or tripped or . . . somehow, she lost her balance and started to lurch forward. Spinning quickly, I caught her, bringing her flush against my body, bracing my feet so we didn't both go down.

She gasped, a slight sound of pain.

"Sorry," I whispered.

Her breathing was slightly elevated, but it wasn't pain in her eyes when I glanced down to meet them, when I smoothed back a lock of dark hair from her forehead.

No, instead, it was heat, her light blue eyes deepening to indigo, her lips parting slightly on an exhale.

My heart began to pound.

Desire arrowed toward my cock, making it grow heavy and hard. God, I'd dreamed about this woman for so long, had wanted her close like this from the moment she'd walked onto the base. Then had been so fucking desperate for it after she'd put herself out there and asked me to dinner. Even when I'd hated it, hated that I could want someone who wasn't my wife, hated that it had reminded me of my fucking failure in that department, I'd wanted her. I'd wanted even as I'd resented desiring anyone else when my personal life had imploded, when it wasn't living up to everything that I had dreamed it could be.

I'd *never* stopped wanting her.

Her mouth parted further, the pink tip of her tongue slipping out to unconsciously moisten her bottom lip.

Then she drifted closer, her breasts pressing against my chest, her hands sliding up the outsides of my arms.

"Olive?" I asked, my voice so fucking hoarse that it sounded like I'd gone five rounds with a flamethrower.

She didn't answer me.

Just lifted on tiptoe and slanted her mouth across mine.

Lightning rod.

That touch was the metal spike on a roof during a storm attracting the electricity in the atmosphere, bringing it down, coalescing it into a huge surge that would level me to the ground.

And the kiss threatened to do just that.

Her lips were soft, and they parted against mine, her tongue sliding along the seam of my mouth, coaxing me into opening, though truthfully, it didn't take much. My nerves were afire with sensation, pulsing desire through my cells, my dick twitching, my hands itching to wrap tightly around her and yank her against me.

But I couldn't do that.

She'd been hurt and—

She'd been hurt.

Fuck. I started to pull back, to release her, to stop kissing her, even though that was the last fucking thing I wanted to do.

But she was still healing.

"Baby," I whispered against her lips, slowing the kiss.

"No," she said, hands coming to my shoulders, keeping me in place. "I need—please, don't stop."

"It's only been a week," I said. "I shouldn't."

She went still, her forehead dropping to my shoulder. "I see." She stepped back, eyes not meeting mine.

"Ollie," I began.

Her gaze drifted up, and the fleeting contact with mine meant that I barely caught a glimpse of those blue eyes before they were gone again.

That glimpse was a fucking gut punch.

"No," I whispered. "It's not—"

"It's okay." A shrug that made her wince. "You don't want me like that or it's too soon or—"

I moved without thinking. One moment I was a foot away from her. The next, she was pressed against the wall, my chest to hers, my body carefully angled away from her injury, one hand on her ass, the other by her head. "No, you don't see," I told her. "You don't understand. I *want* you. I like you. I wouldn't have spent every fucking night at your bedside for the last week if I didn't."

Her exhale coated my lips in hot, damp heat.

Tempting me to put aside my reservations, to kiss her like I so desperately wanted.

But she was hurt.

And I couldn't hurt her again.

I *couldn't*.

"Don't sugarcoat it," she said. "I get it. I'm not"—she waved a hand at her delicious fucking body, as though it weren't the single most luscious, tempting thing I'd ever laid eyes on —"well, I'm not the type of woman who has ever made a man wild with desire and—"

Considering I felt exactly that way—wild, ravenous, needy as fuck—I nearly laughed.

Thankfully, I did have at least a *bit* of experience with women, and I knew something of what it was like for them to reveal an insecurity. And that's what she was doing here. Revealing something, even if she hadn't necessarily wanted to.

Plus, considering I'd been on the other end of revealing just a few days before, I could also sympathize with her.

"You're fucking beautiful," I said, cutting her off before she could disparage herself further. I let my hips rest against hers, let her feel the erection that was pushing at the zipper of my jeans, let her feel how much I wanted her, just from a simple kiss. "I told you, I've wanted you since the moment I laid eyes on you."

Her hands lightly convulsed. "Thank you for saying that." Then her gaze drifted away again, telling me she didn't believe me.

And fuck that.

I dropped my head and kissed her again, still tempering my need, because even though I wanted her quite desperately, I knew I needed to be gentle. But even gentle, it was still the best damned kiss of my life. Her tongue was sure and steady, and it danced with mine. Her hands kneaded my shoulders, nails pricking through the fabric of my shirt. Her moan rumbled up in her chest, vibrated across our mouths, and I swallowed it whole, taking it into me, taking a piece of *her* into me.

And knowing I would never be the same.

This time when we broke apart, my heart was pounding, my fingers were gripping her ass tightly enough that I had to consciously force them to gentle their hold, and the hand on the wall . . . hell, I expected it to have drilled a hole in the wall, considering how tightly it was pressed to the reinforced concrete.

The wall was intact, however.

My control, on the other hand, was tenuous.

"Those fucking sweatpants," I whispered hotly in her ear. "I've seen you wear them around before, you know."

She shook her head.

"They cup your ass like heaven," I said, the words a tempest, swirling around me, lightning strikes in the air, "and I swear to Christ that I've dreamed more times than I should have about picking you up, yanking them down, and plunging home. I can imagine how tight you'd feel, how hot you'd be." I nipped at her throat. "I wouldn't have to be gentle. I could ride you as hard you'd like. And you'd like that, wouldn't you?" I breathed into her ear, feeling her shiver, her body shift closer. "Would like me to fuck you hard, until you screamed my name, until you came around my dick?"

"I—I—"

"Come on, Pops," I said, flicking my tongue out, allowing me a taste of the spicy female scent. "You can do better than that."

She shoved me back. "Fuck off, Linc."

I nipped. "No, I'd rather fuck you."

A laugh, only slightly brittle. "Except, you won't, will you? You may want me, but you won't ever act on it—"

"No," I snapped, pushing back and holding the scorching heat of her gaze. "I won't act on it *tonight*. Because you had a gaping wound in your stomach a fucking week ago. Because you nearly died, and because you don't need me to be pounding into you when you have multiple layers of stitches in your body." I grabbed her arm when she tried to slip by me. "So, no, I won't fuck you tonight."

Her lips parted; her color was high.

I bent until our gazes were even. "But I *will* be fucking you, and I'll be doing it soon."

CHAPTER SEVEN

KTS Satellite Base
Western Georgia
03:59hrs

Olive

"Now," he said, taking my hand. "Let's go take that fucking walk."

I was still reeling from the dirty talk.

Because . . . dirty talk?

Who knew this man had it in him?

I couldn't summon my voice until we were out in the hall, until Linc was towing me away from the infirmary. "You really like when I wear sweats?" I asked.

And really? *That* was the only thing I managed to blurt out? *You like my sweats?*

Gah. It was ridiculous.

But my question was barely out of my lips before I found myself pressed to another wall, his body against every inch of mine—or at least, almost every inch. Because he took care to not press against my still-healing wound, to not jostle me any more than necessary, and *fuck* that melted me into goo. I knew exactly how strong he was, knew what he could do with that body, and yet he was treating me with gentle care.

This man could kill. Easily.

I'd seen it on missions, when our teams had worked together.

He was skilled in hand-to-hand combat. He was strong. He was . . . staring deeply into my eyes and clearing his throat. "*Focus*, Pop."

I frowned. That was the second time today he'd called me that.

But I had to prioritize here. I wanted him to answer my question. "They're just boring gray cotton," I whispered.

A wicked gleam in his eyes, his mouth curving into a sexy smile that actually made my heart skip a beat. "Did you know that gray cotton goes see-through when you bend over?"

I gasped, hands instinctively going to my ass, covering the cheeks. "They don't!"

That wicked gleam intensified. "Oh, no, but they *do*."

My mouth opened and closed. "But why didn't you ever say anything? Why did you—"

"I think my favorite pair of your underwear are the red lacey ones with the cheeky little peek-a-boo."

Cheeks flaring—and *not* the ones he was referring to—I let my stare drift away, looking over his shoulder because . . . oh my God, this was so critically embarrassing.

"I remember the first time I saw them." He laughed. "Fuck, but I practically chased you down the hall and begged you for a glimpse of them without the sweats in the way."

My eyes went back to his. "How many times—?"

I couldn't bring myself to finish the question.

But he knew what I was asking anyway.

"How many times have I seen your panties, Pop?" He tapped a finger to his lips, eyes dancing, then leaned forward and brought his mouth to my ear, his hot breath making me shiver again. "Well, as much as I love the red lace, I do also have a fondness for the butterflies. Oh, and the tiny ones with printed unicorns and the bright pink ones with turquoise bands. Oh and—"

I slapped a hand over his mouth before he could continue listing my entire underwear collection.

And to be frank, it wasn't like I had that many more for him to rattle off.

Lips pressing to my skin, he peeled my hand away and pushed off me. Before I could process the sudden disappointment of losing his body, of wanting him back against me, he was lacing our fingers together and tugging me forward again. "Let's walk, Pop," he said.

"Why the fuck do you keep calling me, Pop?"

"Did you ever notice that when you're distracted, you're more likely to curse?"

I frowned. "What?"

"It's true," he said, leading me around a corner. "I first noticed it when you'd be working on a case that required your full attention. All of a sudden, the f-bombs would be pouring out like water." He brushed his thumb on my wrist, back and forth, back and forth, and goose bumps traveled up my arm, making the skin on my nape prickle and tingle.

I snatched it free. "I don't know what the fuck you're talking about."

"Precisely, Pop."

A sigh. A deep, heavy sigh that had my stitches protesting. "You're not going to tell me why you call me that, are you?"

A beat.

Then, "Nope."

My teeth weren't grinding together. They weren't. They . . . *were*. Not that it mattered. This man was stubborn enough that it wouldn't matter if I continued pressing him. I knew from personal experience, he would just dig in his heels and I would *never* find out why in the hell he was referring to me like a child might refer to their old and wizened grandfather.

Lame.

"Where are we going?"

"A room."

I sighed again.

"Did you know that you make a little growling sound every time you sigh like that?" He took my hand, wove our fingers together again. "It's like a tiny, cute, little kitten snarling at me. I can't help but smile every time you do it."

Now I *really* snarled. "You know what?" I snatched my hand free. "I'm going back to bed."

"But then you'll never find out why I call you Pop."

"You'll never fucking tell me anyway," I snapped.

His lips found mine for a searing kiss that took my breath away, that made my head spin, that had my body drifting against his. Then he lifted his mouth and took my hand again. "You also curse more when you're irritated at me."

I blinked, shook my head to clear it. "That's because you can be really fucking annoying."

Linc just laughed, long and loud, and I couldn't deny that it filled me with warmth. Just the *smallest* amount, because I wasn't a total weakling, but warmth nonetheless, and enough of it that I was towed forward again, until we stopped at a room I hadn't ever been inside. "Do you still want to go back to bed?" he asked, brushing his fingers along my cheek.

"Why?"

"Because we're here."

I glanced at the nondescript door again. "Where's *here*?"

"*Here* is . . ."

Then he opened the door and I swear, I fell a little in love with him right then.

CHAPTER EIGHT

KTS Satellite Base
Western Georgia
04:12hrs

Linc

ONE LOOK AT HER FACE, and I knew I'd done the right thing in bringing her here.

She walked in through the door I'd opened, her mouth dropping open, her eyes going wide. "I—" A shake of her head. "How did you know this was here?"

I shrugged. "I've spent a lot of time on this satellite base."

"Well, I haven't," she whispered. "This is amazing." She crossed over to one of the shelves, running her fingers along the spines of the books stacked upon them. One after another, she walked around the small library and looked at every shelf, rising on tiptoe and bending over enough times that I had to bite back an order for her to just pick a fucking book and sit down.

I knew she was healing rapidly, that the bandage she'd

invented was helping with that process, but I was still itching to protect her—even if that just meant ensuring she got enough rest.

Finally, I couldn't hold that protectiveness back any further. I crossed to her, practically dragged her to the chair, and pushed her down into it. "You tell me which book you want, and I'll grab it for you."

Blue eyes on mine, warmth in their depths. "How did you know I like to read?"

I wanted to tell her that I knew so fucking much about her, that I'd been filing away every detail about her for several years now. But I refrained and simply said, "You've always got some paperback or another in hand."

She smiled, and I would fucking swear that my heart skipped a beat.

I cleared my throat, turned away.

It was either that or launch myself at her, tear off her clothes, and make her and me both very, *very* happy. But, since that wasn't an option at the moment, I needed to find some fucking control.

Fast.

"Mystery?" I asked, crossing to that shelf and pulling out a title I recognized. "I've read this one and enjoyed it."

Silence.

I glanced over my shoulder, saw that she was studying me closely. "What?"

She shook her head.

"Do you want to try this one?"

Another shake of that head.

"No mystery?"

She shrugged.

"What's that mean?"

A slow smile and another shrug, and since I had never seen this woman *not* have a slew of words or preparing to hurl them in my direction, I started to understand that something very fishy was going on here. I slipped the book back into its proper spot, crossed back to her, crouching down to rest my hands on her knees. Her lips parted, a nearly silent exhale filling the air as I moved my hands gently up and down.

"Baby," I whispered. "What do you want to read?"

Her pupils were huge, her lips slightly swollen from our kisses, but the most beautiful part of her was the expression in her eyes—warmth and humor, frolicking around, their arms thrown around each other. Then she smiled, leaned forward slightly, and mischief joined the party. "Why don't you see if you can guess correctly?"

I bent toward her until our mouths were almost touching, until I could feel the damp warmth of her breath on my lips. "What do I get if I do?"

Fire licking at the edges of her blue eyes, pink tinging her cheeks, her breaths increasing. "Is that what this is about?" A raised eyebrow. "Tit for tat?"

Another lean, this time moving closer until my lips brushed hers as I spoke. "You said *tit*."

She froze. Then leaned back and glared at me, her second brow joining the first. "Seriously?"

I tugged a lock of her long brown hair. "Yup. Plus, I happen to like your tits, so you've got that going for you."

She swatted at me, but I was already dancing back.

"All right," I said, perusing the shelves, scanning the titles as I put together my plan, however devious it might turn out to be. All was fair in love and war, right? And I intended to win this particular war. Olive was mine.

Even if she didn't know it.

"All right, what?"

"All right, I'll see if I can guess correctly." I turned to face her, leaning against the wall. "But we need to set some parameters first."

She groaned. "God, not you and your fucking parameters."

I grinned. "Last I checked, you seemed to love to do battle with me and my parameters."

"Only because you have a million of them. And that should be fucking hyperbole, but it's not. Because I swear to fucking God that every single project we work on together, it's always, *We need to consider this angle* and *We can't move forward until we account for all of these variables*." She tossed up her hands. "You'd talk and plan and consider until the day you died if I didn't push you to act."

That was true in some aspects.

I *did* plan and plot, sometimes to an extreme degree.

But that planning and plotting were going to be to her bene-fit. Because I was going to win this woman over, and we were going to be blissfully happy together, dammit.

I also knew that the cursing told me she was distracted.

By what though?

Surreptitiously, I glanced around the small room, noting that nothing was out of place. Next, I made sure she was okay. She didn't look uncomfortable or cold, at least not in that moment. Instead, her color was high, and her eyes were locked on . . . my stare flicked down, and I saw my shirt had lifted, revealing a strip of my abdomen.

I bit back a grin.

All right then.

I could work with that.

Shifting so the gap widened, I slipped my thumbs into the pockets of my jeans, knowing the weight would draw the waist-band down slightly.

The pink tip of her tongue darted out to moisten her bottom lip.

Her gaze was heavy, an almost tangible stroke across my skin.

My cock twitched, my control slipped, and I knew I couldn't play this game any longer, not if I wanted to keep my plan in place. Clearing my throat as I straightened, my hands slipping free, my shirt and jeans shifting back into place—I probably looked like the most fidgety teenager of all time—I said, "Okay, well, my *parameters* for this little guessing game of yours are as follows—and let it be noted that I will be open to your changes and additions *after* I've laid them out—"

"Oh, my God," she groaned, making me lose my battle with my smile. "This isn't a policy discussion."

No. It was more than that.

It was the first step to winning her heart.

So, one might say it was the most important *policy* discussion of my life.

"One," I said, ignoring her groaning. "I'll have three guesses. *Two*," I added louder when she didn't immediately stop with the grousing, "if I guess correctly, then you'll grant me one ask."

"What do you mean by *ask*?"

A shrug. "I mean, I'll ask you a question, and you'll answer it truthfully."

She made a face. "I can't commit to that without knowing the question."

"Uh-hum. No changes or additions until I've laid out my considerations, remember?" I said, instead of committing to that.

Her mouth gaped. "You have *more*?"

"Just one more," I said then cleared my throat again, as though I were issuing a very important proclamation . . . and I supposed I was. "Three, you'll agree to go on a date with me, on a day, time, and at a location of my choosing."

Silence. Then a question in a very formal tone to match mine. "Is that your last condition?"

I nodded, still serious. "Yup, just those three."

Her finger lifted, tapping her chin, and I just watched her, mesmerized by the way the lights shining overhead made her dark hair shimmer and shine, turned her skin golden and tempting, like a shining statue I was desperate to run my fingers over. But then the statue moved, shifting in that graceful, sinuous way of hers, and it was impossible to fully comprehend this living, breathing beauty with the stillness she embodied at times. How could she be both so full of life and yet still so even, so quiet, so self-contained?

Except with me.

I seemed to manage to get under her skin.

A card I was duty-bound to play.

Because I was *playing* for keeps.

Finally, she seemed to come to a decision, shifting again in the chair, and I didn't miss her wince.

A blip of worry. "Are you uncomfortable?" I glanced around the library, spotted a basket of throw pillows and blankets and grabbed one of each. "Do you want this behind your back? Are you cold?" Fingers circling my wrist, halting my flow of questions, one hand taking the pillow and shifting so she could tuck it behind her back. I spread the blanket over her legs, crouched down again, well aware that she could have been a queen and me her subject kneeling at her feet.

But I didn't care.

Because when I finished smoothing the blanket, she cupped my cheek. "I'll agree to the three guesses. I'll agree to *consider* answering the question." I parted my lips, ready to protest, and she smiled, shook her head. "My turn for parameters, remember?"

I made a face. "I remember."

Her laughter—never soft and tinkling, but full-bodied and strong—coated my skin like honey, sticking to my limbs, seeping inside, filling my heart with joy that matched hers.

"You'll listen?"

More face-making. "If I *have* to."

Amusement flickering on the edges of her expression, she tapped me lightly on the nose. "There now, that wasn't so hard, was it?"

"Careful," I growled, snagging her hand and pressing a kiss to the inside of her wrist.

Blue eyes dimming slightly. "I'm always careful." A pause. "Well, *almost* always." Her lips pressed flat, released, going plump and kissable again, her tone clearly telling me that she wasn't going to be open to me pushing her for more information about whatever the fuck *that* meant.

I had patience in spades.

I knew that trust would come all in good time.

But I fucking hated that she didn't trust me enough to tell me all the heavy shit, the sad shit, the *bad* shit. I wanted to know every bit, to shoulder it, to make it less burdensome for her, even as I knew that I hadn't yet earned that right.

"I'll consider answering the question," she repeated, the statement's manner telling me there would be no negotiating on that front. Which was fine, I'd just need to be very careful with what I asked and to make it count. "Last, for the date . . ." Her gaze trailed up, met mine, holding for several moments. "Are you sure that you're ready to do that?" She swallowed. "I mean . . . it hasn't been that long since I asked and—"

I covered her hand with mine. "I'm sure."

Brown brows pulling together. "*That's* it?"

"That's it," I told her. "I meant it when I told you a few days ago that I was coming to apologize before the explosion. I've thought of little else over the last few months except how much of a dick I was to you." I shoved a hand through my hair. "That was a wake-up call for me. I didn't like the person I'd become, hated that I'd hurt you." My hand dropped to my side. "That moment, realizing what I'd done, who I was becoming . . . it had me planning my apology to you ever since."

She inhaled, let it out slowly. "Oh."

My mouth twitched. "*That's* it?"

Eyes narrowing into a mock glare, she sat back on the chair like it was her throne. "You're not funny."

"Your laughter would tell me otherwise."

More mock glaring. "Hmm." Then she waved a hand before steepling both in front of her chin. "Commence with the guessing already."

"Feeling like a queen?" I teased, thinking she'd embraced my earlier thought fully.

"More like a king," she said. "Or some all-powerful, gender-neutral ruler who has minions kneeling at her feet." She mimed putting on a crown. "Now, I just need a scepter."

Chuckling, I stood and reached into the corner, tossing her the dusting rod that someone had left there. "Here you go."

"Ah, thank you, minion."

Smile huge, laughter bubbling in my chest, I ignored the urge to move back to her, to continue teasing each other, and to see the way her eyes danced with humor when I scored a particularly good one-liner.

Instead, I made my way to the romance shelf.

Because I'd been paying attention to the paperbacks she'd been carrying around. Because I knew she read these books with their colorful covers (and sexy man chests) and guaranteed happy endings. I also knew she had her favorites.

I'd seen her carrying those tattered paperbacks around, spines creased from re-reads. I'd noted them on her desk, stacked along one edge, or stuffed into the side pocket of her cargos.

I'd paid attention.

I'd deduced her favorite authors.

One of whom had a book that had been released just a few days before.

Said book happened to find its way to this shelf for this exact reason. Not that I'd expected it to be tonight, I'd just . . . been plotting and planning for the opportunity to give it to her.

A KTS agent knew when to be prepared, knew when to lay charges in advance, knew that planning often saved missions from going FUBAR.

And tonight, my planning would come into play.

But because I had three guesses, I couldn't resist playing with her. Just a *little* bit. I bypassed the romance section, walked straight to the shelf with the military history tomes, and picked up the oldest, heaviest one I could find. Then I walked it back over to Olive. "This one," I said, plunking it into her lap.

She grabbed at the book before it could slide from her lap. "*History of Ammunitions circa 1916-1928.*" Her eyes met mine, mouth tipped up at the corners. "You shouldn't have," she added dryly.

"It's a fascinating read—"

"No," she interrupted. "What's *fascinating* is the fact that you somehow think that I don't know you're messing with me."

I laughed, snagged the book, and put it back in its spot. "I couldn't resist."

"Your funeral," she said. "And now, you only have two guesses left."

"Hmm." I tapped my fingers across the shelves. "Decisions, decisions."

"You know, you didn't specify what would happen when you blew your three chances. What's *my* consolation prize?"

I grabbed another laughable book—this one about yak migration through Nepal—and moved back to the chair, handing it over. "You didn't negotiate for a consolation prize."

She glanced at the title then up at me. "You're kidding me, right?"

I just grinned.

"There is no way this is an actual book," she said, running her fingers over the cover. "You've seriously got to be kidding me."

I snagged it back, returned it to the shelf, and this time . . . I made my play, grabbing the new release, carefully hiding the cover as I returned to the chair again. "What do you want for a consolation prize?"

Playful blue eyes, fingertips tapping together in a very

going-to-take-over-the-world type of way. "Oh, man, the possibilities are absolutely endless. What torture should I enact?"

"You could always kiss me," I pointed out.

Those lush lips curved up. "And where's the torture in that?"

"It's *torture* because I know that I can't do anything more than kiss you"—I ran my free hand along the outside of her arm, my fingertips brushing the outer curve of her breast—"even though I'm quite desperate to do so much more than that."

"*Quite* desperate?" she asked.

I nodded, repeated the motion with my hand, only this time moving up instead of down. "*Quite* is a small word for what I want to do with you."

She shivered. "So, kissing as my consolation prize." Her voice was barely more than a murmur, but the heat in her eyes was palpable. "I suppose that I can consider torturing you a reasonable prize."

"Well," I said, still hiding the book. "You'd better take your consolation prize now."

Her brows lifted. "You're not even going to try for a third time?"

I shrugged.

"Never thought of you as a quitter." She leaned forward in the chair, brought her mouth within a hairsbreadth of mine. "Okay then," she said. "Let the torture begin." And then her mouth came to mine.

Fire.

Licking down my spine, spreading throughout my limbs, reducing my control to cinders.

All just from her lips on mine, from her tongue dancing alongside mine, her moan vibrating through our mouths, drifting through my body until it sank into my cells. Her hands came up to grip my shoulders, to bring me closer, and . . . I could just keep kissing this woman for an eternity.

But we needed to breathe.

I drew back, smoothed my hand along her cheek, sitting back on my heels, and . . . deposited the book I'd kept hidden on her lap.

She felt the weight, glanced down.

Then burst into tears.

CHAPTER NINE

KTS Satellite Base
Western Georgia
04:46hrs

Olive

HECK if I knew why I was crying, except to say that it seemed like everything hit me, all at once.

The explosion. The pain. The fear. This man. His words.

And . . . the fucking book.

All of it weighed heavy on me, sinking down into my heart, seeping into my abdomen, cluttering up my mind . . .

And I lost it.

Just full-on burst into tears.

Look, I was a woman who didn't have a problem crying. Give me a sad article or news story, a cheesy romcom, or one of those SPCA commercials, and I became a freaking watering pot.

But in the *real* world?

When shit got stressful and people were hurt, when situations were dangerous—or *not*. In the course of a normal freaking day, where normal things were happening, where normal people were interacting . . . I absolutely *never* had meltdowns.

I was even, steady—whether it was life or death, or just . . . life.

But somehow, give me a half hour with this man, his care, his banter, the way he looked at me, and a freaking book I'd been dying to read, and I was practically drowning in my own tears and snot.

Because I was not a cute, dainty crier.

I was swollen eyes and a running nose. I was tear tracks and hitching sobs. I was . . .

Being lifted into a set of strong arms.

Linc scooped me up then took my spot in the chair, gently turning me so I was situated in his lap. And then he just held me, running his hand lightly through my hair, not saying a word as I cried for reasons unbeknownst to myself.

"I wondered when this was going to happen," he whispered.

Sniffing loudly—because circling back to ugly crying and snot and tears—I pushed lightly against his chest until I could see his face. "What do you mean?"

"You nearly died, Pop." His hand didn't stop tracing those gentle patterns. "Most people have this reaction sooner or later."

"Snot?" I asked, wiping my face unceremoniously on my sleeve. If the man had a problem with my personal hygiene, then he could suck it. It wasn't like I had a box of tissues in my pocket.

He didn't comment about my snot.

Instead, he just kept stroking my back as he reached into his pocket and pulled out a packet of tissues. He handed it to me, and I spent the next few moments wiping my eyes and nose.

With actual tissues.

Because this man . . .

"How did you know about the book?" I whispered.

He shrugged, a difficult feat with me in his arms. "I pay attention."

"Linc," I began.

"Do you want to read here?" he asked. "Or take it back to the infirmary?"

"Linc," I said again.

"How are you—" I struggled for a moment. "The book—" A shake of my head. "The tears. The *tissues*—" God, I felt my eyes start to well again. Maybe it *was* just because of the explosion, being near death. Except . . . this outburst of emotion felt like more.

Like I was standing on the precipice and looking over that edge, terrified to leap, yet knowing I was going to hop over anyway.

"It's simple, baby. I pay attention," he whispered. Then his voice strengthened, returned to his normal crisp tone. "Now, do you want to read here or the infirmary?"

And I found I could return to normal, too. Or at least some semblance of it. "Neither."

His brows furrowed.

I lifted my chin. "I want to read in my own bed, without people coming in and out, without interruptions, with *real* rest —not rest in a hospital room."

A shake of his head. "I can't discharge you, yet."

I rolled my eyes. "Why not?"

"Because—"

"I've been checking my own chart, you know," I muttered. "It's not like I can't see that I'm ready to be recuperating in my quarters. I was going to push the issue tomorrow, or rather today," I added.

"Well, I'm not letting you go back to your rooms alone."

I scowled.

His eyes held a thread of emotion I couldn't distinguish. "So, you'll just have to come with me to mine."

My mouth dropped open. *"What?"*

But he was already on his feet, with me still in his arms. I grabbed the book before it could fall, held on as best I could as he shifted to open the door, and then we were in the hall, and he was still carrying me as he walked.

"Um—"

"Infirmary or my bed," he said.

"Um," was still all I could manage.

Pick a step, Olive, I counseled myself. *First, walk on your own. Then an argument about sleeping arrangements.*

"Pop," he warned.

"Put me down."

He ignored me, kept walking, using his key card to open a door I knew led to sleeping quarters. They weren't where my team and I were housed, but the layout was familiar enough. A long corridor, doors on either side that led to small sets of rooms, each with their own bedroom, kitchenette, living area, and bathroom.

"I thought you were giving me a choice."

"I was," he said. "Until you didn't make one." His eyes met mine, brows flicking up in a gesture daring me to argue, and I knew I *should* have argued, just like I should have pressed for him to put me down. But after my late-night walk, and the time in the library, and my crying fit, frankly, I was exhausted.

So, I let him carry me to his rooms, and I didn't say another damned word about it.

He set me on the bed . . . also something I didn't say anything about, nor did I complain when he tucked the blankets around me, when he turned on the small lamp next to the bed.

I did, however, complain when he toed off his shoes and then started to make himself comfortable in the armchair, his phone in hand as he stared at the screen.

"Hey."

He looked up.

I jumped over that cliff.

Also known as, I patted the bed next to me. "Come here."

His brows rose again, and this time it was an, "Are you serious?" flick of those dark brown strips of hair.

I nodded.

And a moment later, he was in bed.

Next to me.

My heart rate galloped through my veins and arteries. My palms went sweaty, almost making me lose my grip on the book.

"Okay?" he whispered.

I nodded again. This time because I was unable to form words. He was just so . . . *much*, and I felt panic lick at the edges of my mind. What in the hell was I doing? I was in his room, in his bed. I'd forgiven him for hurting my feelings a few months back, but was I really doing *this*? Was I really going to jump, to hurl myself over the cliff? That was dangerous and stupid and—

"Is it everything you hoped it would be?"

I blinked.

His eyes were filled with humor, his brows waggling, and I couldn't help but relax, laughter slipping out of me to fill the room. It was too loud, too much, and I started to lift a hand to my mouth, to stifle it.

Linc caught it. "Don't."

I looked at him questioningly.

"I love your laugh," he murmured. "Don't hide it."

"Oh." But I wasn't laughing now. I was touched, the panic a forgone thought.

"Yeah. *Oh.*" He smoothed back my hair, shifting on the mattress. It was only a full-sized, so it wasn't like there was a *ton* of room to maneuver—something I probably should have considered before inviting him to lie next to me. I hadn't, of course, so we both ended up dancing around each other as we both tried to get enough space to be comfortable.

A minute later, I had my head on his shoulder and my book propped on his chest, and we were . . . lying in bed together.

How was this even a thing?

"Read your book," he murmured, a couple of minutes later, when I'd just lain there like a statue continuing to wonder how it *was* a thing, how I'd ended up in this bed with this man, invitation or not.

I obeyed.

Not because he'd given me the order.

But because I'd waited six months for this book, and it was finally in my hot, little hands, and I wanted to read it.

Now.

And it was just as good as I'd hoped, as I'd wanted it to be.

———

I AWOKE on a slightly rumbling male chest.

My mouth was dry, throat scratchy, and it felt like I'd slept a dozen hours. I shifted slightly to look at the clock on the nightstand and saw that it had actually been *fourteen* hours.

The book was on the nightstand, with what looked like a receipt marking the page where I must have dozed off, and it seemed that I'd stolen all the covers.

Linc's bare feet were poking out at the bottom, and there was something sexy about male feet—or at least, about *this* male's feet, because they weren't gross looking, just strong and competent—could feet be competent? Probably not, but also, this just in . . . I was losing my mind, waxing poetic about strong, *competent* feet.

Next, those feet would have a sense of humor to go along with all that strength and competence and—

Enough.

I'd been curled up on my good side, but my wound was throbbing from the position anyway.

Carefully, I shifted, rolling flat on my back and waiting for the burning to subside. Which, thankfully, didn't take long. I was definitely healing, and even though I was ready to be done with the whole process, I knew my progress to date had been remarkable. Now, I just needed to behave and take it easy, just as I always ordered my patients to do.

Rest. Don't push it. Let my body recuperate.

The trouble was the advice was a lot harder to accept than it was to dish out.

I wanted to find out who'd planted the bomb—was it Daniel? Was it someone else? Did we have another traitor? Or had an enemy somehow managed to penetrate our defenses?

Normally, I would be in on all of the briefings to understand what had happened, instead of stuck in a hospital bed. But I *had* been stuck in a bed, and I would probably be stuck there for most of my immediate future. Small bursts of activity, then back to bed. Maybe up for a meal or two, then lying down to rest again.

For someone like me, who thrived on being busy, on working on a dozen projects at once, the idea of forced rest was a difficult pill to swallow.

I would take it, of course.

Because I knew it was the proper treatment for my recovery —along with keeping the wound clean, watching for any sign of infection, and then eventually taking the sutures out.

But I was definitely going to groan and gripe about it in my head.

Terrible. The whole thing was *terrible*.

The other terrible thing?

I had to get out of this warm and cozy bed to use the facilities.

I didn't *wanna!* And yet, this was another one of those things that I was just going to have shut up and do. Adulting sucked, as much as being sidelined when the rest of my team wasn't— okay, that wasn't exactly true. Dan and Ava would be on base recovering for near about the same time as I would be.

The reality was that the majority of my team was on rest.

Laila and Ryker were the only two on our team who were

actively working to investigate the attack. But I also knew that Dan and Ava had been reviewing the latest files on the Mikhailova clan. They'd told me the last time they'd visited. So, I guess that brought me back to the whole sidelined thing.

Ugh.

I needed to find something to keep me busy that wasn't going to put my recovery at risk.

But first . . . the bathroom.

Slipping out from beneath Linc's arm, I slid the covers back and carefully sat up, wincing both at the pull of my stitches and also at the cold floor on my sock-covered feet.

Chilly.

The man liked to keep his room chilly.

Not that I minded so much, when I was able to cuddle up with that warm body of his. It, however, did certainly make for some very large temperature swings.

Scorching desert to frozen tundra in the span of a few seconds.

Good times.

I crept toward the bathroom, moving as silently as possible so as not to wake Linc. He'd been pulling enough hours in the infirmary to make a normal man cry and then add in the extra time he'd spent with me, and he needed his rest as much as I did.

"Where do you think you're going?"

I jumped, one hand coming to my chest, pressing over my pounding heart. The other instinctively resting against my stitches.

But no pain came from the movement.

More progress.

Though less of making it to the bathroom.

"I'll be right back," I said, turning to see him in bed, his T-shirt wrinkled, his hair mussed. He wiped a hand across his sleepy eyes as I said, "I just need to use the facilities."

"Facilities?" His hand dropped, and just like the agent and

doctor he was, Linc's gaze had already been cleared of sleep. Immediately awake in just a few heartbeats. "Pop," he said, a hint of a growl in his voice. "What are you doing?"

I huffed, one hand dropping to my hip. "I have to pee, okay?"

"Okay." He smiled. "So long as you come back and cuddle up next to me when you're done."

My cheeks felt hot, and I wanted, really wanted to have a quick quip ready on the tip of my tongue to fling over my shoulder at him. Unfortunately, I couldn't come up with anything. So instead, I just hurried into the bathroom, shut and locked the door, did my business, washed my hands, and—

There was a knock at the door.

"Y-yes?" I answered.

"Extra toothbrush in the second drawer on the right. If you need to shower, I have a waterproof wrapping in the cabinet behind you. Girly hair shit also in that cabinet."

"Thanks," I said, bending to retrieve the wrapping as I chuckled at the "girly hair shit" line.

For a moment.

Then I realized what it meant.

He had offered up another woman's hair products. Did that mean he'd dated someone else at the base? Did that mean there *was* someone else?

My mind revolted.

He wouldn't do that. He was a good guy and—

There was another knock.

"If you look at the labels, you'll see they're your brand, baby." A beat. "Because I pay attention."

My heart settled, and I was able to take a full breath.

"Be careful in the shower."

"Thanks," I murmured, knowing he couldn't hear me.

"You're welcome, Pop," he said, as though he had.

And maybe he had; the man *was* practically a superhero after all.

CHAPTER TEN

KTS Satellite Base
Western Georgia
19:02hrs

Linc

SHE WAS GETTING NAKED, just on the other side of a flimsy wooden door.

Or, maybe not *flimsy* per se.

All the doors at KTS were made of a specialized concrete polymer, similar to that of the garage, designed to withstand bullets and explosions. So, I may not be able to burst through the locked door with my shoulder, to kick it in with a splintering of hinges.

But I could pretend to know what she was saying.

What she was thinking.

Because—everybody in the back join me in saying—*I pay attention.*

I didn't want her thinking that I bought the products for another woman, not when I'd gone to great lengths to understand her preferences, to sneak in the girly shit so my team wouldn't see them and ferret onto what was happening.

If they did . . .

Oh man, the amount of shit I would get—

A shake of my head.

I knew it was going to get dished out, sooner or later, but I definitely wasn't looking forward to it.

Regardless, I also knew that shit-giving would absolutely be worth it.

Even if I was having to exercise even more self-control by not attempting to barrel that door down, no matter how fruitless my efforts would turn out to be.

To distract myself, I spent the next few minutes changing my clothes, ordering some room service—there were occasional perks to being a KTS agent, and one of those was free twenty-four-hour-a-day food delivery. Great for those on shift who couldn't make it to the mess or for those recovering from the various injuries they sustained on the job.

Or for those who wanted to avoid the gossiping eyes of the rest of the base.

At least for a few more minutes.

There was nothing to be done for my breath—my mouth felt like I had swallowed an entire desert—but I shoved in a couple of pieces of gum to tie me over until I could hit up the bathroom and my toothbrush in that drawer.

Then I brewed some coffee, knowing the lure of caffeine would coax Olive out of the shower sooner rather than later.

She lived for the brew, downing more of it than I would have thought possible for such a small woman. And more than enough to make me jittery. Still, the lure worked before long, Olive appearing in the hall with a towel wrapped around her luscious body and her hair a wet sheet down her back.

I almost missed the rueful expression.

"What?" I asked.

A blush. "I couldn't bear to put my dirty clothes back on."

Fucking hell, it would be so easy to nudge that towel to the floor. Instead of that, however, I spun back to my dresser and yanked out a T-shirt and pair of sweats, passing them over to her.

She disappeared back into the bathroom at the same time there was a knock on the door. Answering it, I started to snag the tray, wanting to get some food into Olive so she could keep up her strength. My fingers grasped the plastic tray, my mind on what I could coax Pop into after I'd done my part to keep up her strength, and my eyes not really taking in who was on the other side of that concrete panel.

Until I heard, "Eating for an army, Doc?"

I focused on the voice, saw it was Jack holding the tray, his eyes going wide, a trace of something in them that had my hackles rising, but before I could ferret that feeling out, all I could think was . . . "*Shiiit.*"

Because precisely at that moment, Olive came out of the bathroom, my sweats in her hand, my T-shirt hitting her mid-thigh, her hair still sleek and hanging in a damp sheet on her back, announcing, "Your sweats were too big, so I decided to go . . ." Her eyes went to the door. ". . .without," she finished, and God, how was it possible for a human's cheeks to go so pink?

I snatched the tray, slammed the door in my teammate's face, then turned to face her. "I'm sure he won't say anything."

I wasn't sure of that at all.

Hell, I was pretty damned sure it would be the opposite, but she looked so embarrassed—*no.* Embarrassed was a mild term for it. In fact, she looked like she was going to run screaming from the room. Which meant, I knew I'd say whatever it took to prevent that.

Not that my words seemed to have the effect I'd planned—read: she didn't look consoled or comforted, not in the least—but, surprisingly, I did catch amusement edging into the lines of her face.

"Of course, he's going to be blabbing about this to anyone

and everyone." She pressed her palms to her cheeks, as though that would make the swathe of pink go away. "I sure as hell would, if I'd gotten this scoop." Her voice turned announcer. "This just in! Two doctors who hate each other have been found in the bedroom of one. Clothing may have been removed, and panties were certainly optional."

I froze, then moved to set the tray down. "Are they?"

She frowned. "Are they what?"

I crossed back over to her, fingers drawn to the silken skin of her bare thighs. "Are your panties optional?" I drew light circles near the hem of that shirt, dipping underneath, loving the way her breath hitched, desperate to trace them higher, even as I knew I shouldn't.

If I went higher, I would be even more tempted than I was before, and—

Fingers circling my wrist.

I thought to pull away.

Instead, those fingers were tugging my hand higher.

And suddenly my fingers were against molten, wet heat.

"Considering I wasn't wearing any to begin with—something you should have noticed since you seem to be appraised of my see-through sweats situation—yes," she said. "Yes, they're optional."

My fingers slid through the heat, and I watched her lips part, her eyes darken. "I thought you were wearing a nude pair," I said, somehow able to form words. *Somehow* because my heart was galloping, my pulse pounding in my ears, the rapid *thrum-thrum* making it hard to hear, hard to focus.

"I don't own any nude pairs," she murmured, her feet shifting, her thighs spreading apart.

I dipped a finger between the folds of her pussy, watched her eyes glaze over. "No?"

A shake of her head. "I—ah—only buy colorful pairs," she said, hips jerking as I slowly circled her clit. "It's nice to—" She broke off when I lightly tapped the bundle of nerves, pressing down and returning to my circling, her knees almost buckling, her body leaning heavily against mine.

I kept with the rhythm.

Pressure. Circling. She liked that. *A lot.*

Noted.

I held her against me and continued stroking. "It's nice to what?"

"I—" A shake of her head, her cheek coming to a rest against my chest. "I have no idea what you're talking about."

Stopping my fingers, I said, "You were telling me why you only buy colorful underwear."

Heavy-lidded eyes blinked. "I was?"

This woman was so fucking sexy. "You were."

"Oh." A shrug, more blinking, her pupils so wide there was only a narrow strip of light blue visible. "I like color." Another shrug. "And we don't often get to wear it."

"And the lace?" I asked, slowly moving again.

"The lace is for me." A beat, her lips curving into a hot, sexy smile. "And maybe because I imagined you peeling them off me."

My rhythm faltered. My cock went somehow harder, and I stopped playing around. I scooped her up into my arms, carried her to the bed, still coherent enough to set her down gently, rather than tossing her on the mattress and pouncing on top of her. "Lace," I said, kissing the inside of her ankle. "I'm going to buy you more lace."

"Mmm." She hissed out air when I nipped at one thigh then the other.

"And then I'm going to spend a fuck-ton of time peeling it off you."

"Sounds— Good—*ah*—"

I traced my tongue up that soft skin, moved toward the damp heat of her. She smelled sweet and spicy, my soap mixed with the scent that was intrinsically Olive. It was a fucking drug. It made me desperate and needy—to touch, to kiss, to plunge deep.

I couldn't do that last right now.

But the first two, I could do.

And I was going to enjoy them a hell of a lot.

I nudged her legs further apart, bent my head, and found that rhythm . . . only this time, it was with my tongue. My hands were otherwise occupied, one pulling her hips against my mouth, keeping the contact so I could find that rhythm. The other sliding up her abdomen, carefully avoiding her bandage as I made my way to her breasts. I'd made a critical error in not peeling off the shirt, the fucking material blocking what would certainly be the best view of my life, but she was bucking against my tongue, sexy little moans pouring out of her mouth, so I wasn't going to stop what I was doing with mine.

Even though seeing her naked breasts was right up there with the things I wanted most in the world.

1. End child hunger.
2. Enact world peace.
3. See Olive Jacobs' breasts.

And I didn't mean to see them in a clinical setting, because I couldn't lie and say I *hadn't* seen them before. I'd caught glimpses of many naked bodies. But I always looked away. First, because I was a professional. Second, because I wasn't a fucking scumbag. I didn't prey upon people when they were vulnerable.

So yeah, I wanted a glimpse of those breasts in this venue.

I also wanted to get my mouth on them, to feel the nipples bead against my tongue. To kiss every inch of silky skin, to rub the stubble of my jaw against the undersides, to trace patterns with my lips. I wanted—

Well, suffice to say, I wanted to spend some serious quality time with those breasts.

But, for now, I had my mouth on Olive's wet pussy, had the tart and sweet mix of her on my tongue, and she was moaning my name.

I would be staying right where I was for the foreseeable future.

Which meant I had to satisfy myself with just touching her breasts, with cupping them, with plucking and rolling the nipples in time to the movement of my tongue.

"Linc—" she whispered.

"Hmm?" I asked, never lifting my lips.

"I—I—I need—" Her head flopped back onto the pillows; her thighs tightened around my shoulders. "I *need* — "

I shifted, slipped a finger deep, curling it up, finding that sensitive spot deep inside.

She moaned. "That. Yes, *that.*" Her legs squeezed around my shoulders again, her hips jerking as she ground herself against my mouth—

And then she came on my tongue.

Fuck that was good, watching her eyes slide closed, her lips parting on a loud, slow groan. Her body went ramrod stiff for long moments until she slumped against the bed, chest rising and falling in rapid intervals. I kissed her gently, slowly bringing her down from the peak, before crawling up her body, careful to keep my weight off her and pressing my mouth lightly against hers.

My cock was ready to snap in half, but I couldn't be anything but content as I took her into my arms.

"That was—" She shook her head, laughed slightly. "Long overdue."

I smiled down at her. "Trust me, I was thinking the same."

She rolled over, rested her folded arms on my chest, a satisfied smile on her face. "Have you planned very much?"

I stroked a hand over her hair. "What do you think?"

She laughed. "That it's a yes."

"It's a yes," I agreed.

"Linc?"

"Hmm?" I was too distracted stroking my hands over her skin to catch the glimmer of wicked in her eyes. Which was probably why it took me a few moments to process exactly where her hand was going.

But I certainly didn't miss it cupping me through my jeans.

I groaned, hips jerking up.

She reached for the zipper.

I brushed her hands away. "Not today, Pop," I said. "I already feel guilty enough for debauching you. Don't let me add my own selfishness to the mix."

Her fingers crept back, stroked along the length of my cock. "Me wanting to touch you isn't selfish—or at least, not selfish on your part." Lips curving as she tugged the tag of my zipper. "My part, however? *Definitely.* I can't wait to get my hands on you."

Oh, sweet baby Jesus.

I slid down the mattress, bringing my lips in line with hers, kissing her until I could hardly see straight.

And then I slipped from the bed.

She laughed, unperturbed by my fleeing. "You're more stubborn than I am."

I shrugged. "Maybe."

"I want it noted for the record that the only reason you're winning this particular argument is because I'm injured and slow."

"Maybe," I said again and moved to the tray. "Now, come eat."

More laughter, but she slowly pushed up from the bed, making her way to the table as I set out plates of lukewarm pasta. "This is more of you taking care of me?" she asked as I put a bowl of salad in front of both plates.

I paused, glanced over at her. "Take it as you wish."

Blue eyes on mine, holding for long moments.

Then she nodded . . . and reached onto the tray to put a piece of bread on my plate.

I didn't miss the small gesture for what it was.

She was taking care of me right back.

Yeah, a man could get used to that.

CHAPTER ELEVEN

KTS Satellite Base
Western Georgia
10:36hrs

Olive

I WINCED, HISSING OUT A BREATH. "EASY," I warned.

Linc glanced up from where he was taking out my stitches.

I'd discovered a drawback to my fancy bandages. They healed a little too fast. Which meant that the stitches probably should have been taken out the night before instead of this morning.

But I'd been so comfy in Linc's arms that it had slipped my mind.

We'd gorged ourselves on pasta, salad, and bread, and then he'd put on one of my absolute favorite movies, *Die Hard.*

How the man had discovered so much about me was a freaking mystery. He just kept telling me that he paid attention, but it couldn't simply be that. I'd dated plenty of men, and I could count on one hand—hell, on one *finger*—those that could remember my middle name, let alone my favorite movie or author.

Linc was different.

He seemed to know me better than I knew myself.

And I'd just stopped hating him, what . . . four? Five? Days ago?

Hate or love—well, *like*—didn't matter. Because I was really hating what was happening on my side right now.

That being, the stitches, partially overgrown, having to be tugged out of my skin.

I cursed as he removed another, clenching my fingers into the sheet and trying not to smack his hand away so I could just do it myself. I knew he was trying to be gentle, knew it wasn't his fault.

But . . . fucking hell, that hurt.

"Come on," he said, slowly working on the next one. "You ladies wax your hoo-hahs. This can't be that bad in comparison."

"Waxing," I said, gritting my teeth, "isn't this fucking slow. It's one rip and done."

He paused, glanced up at me. "You want me to rip your skin out?"

"No—I mean, *yes*." I gestured with one hand to my side. "No, skin. Yes, rip faster."

"I'm trying *not* to hurt you."

I snatched the tweezers. "Give it here," I muttered.

He handed me the small pair of scissors, and I noticed he was trying to bite back a smile.

"What?" I snapped as I went to work on the few remaining sutures.

"I just knew that sooner or later, you wouldn't be able to resist taking the job over for yourself."

I winced as I made quick work of the remaining few stitches, going with the snip and rip method rather than the slow, inexorable tug that Linc seemed to have perfected. And, frankly, by the time I'd finished with the last one, I wasn't sure whose method was better.

But the stitches were out.

I could resume normal duties—sort of. Light duties were going to be my speed for the next little while.

Which was fine. I'd be able to at least do something more productive than just lazing about.

"Here." My eyes drifted to Linc, watching as he gathered the trash and put the sharps into a bin to be disinfected. Then he came back over, bending a little in order to stare at my side. "I think one more day with a fresh bandage, and you'll be good to go back to light duty."

Since I had just been thinking the same thing, I only nodded in response.

"What do you have planned for today?" he asked, as though we hadn't just spent the better part of the last day in each other's arms discussing everything under the sun, including my desire to go back to work.

"I'm going to catch up on paperwork," I said. "I've seen quite a few files cross my inbox but haven't been in the right mental headspace to actually process them."

"I'm sure your entire team is going to be raring to go once Ava and Dan get cleared."

"That's probably the understatement of the year."

He smiled. "Can I see you tonight?"

"Are you calling in your marker for our one date?"

"No."

I pushed up from the bed, found my feet, ignoring his steadying hand on my arm. I was feeling a little prickly and wanted to brush it away, but I knew that was just because I was feeling off-center.

This man had stormed into my life in the last week, and he was wonderful, and part of me just wanted to get swept up in all that wonderful.

But my experience had taught me that all the wonderful didn't last.

Hell, *his* experience should have taught him that.

And maybe it had. Maybe he just had more courage than me, was willing to potentially get hurt again. And . . . maybe I wasn't.

"Slow, Pop."

I blinked, glancing up from where I'd paused, my feet on the floor, my butt resting on the edge of the bed in the infirmary. "What?"

He leaned next to me. "We've got plenty of time." His fingers came to mine, lacing them together and lifting my hand so he could kiss the back of it. "This doesn't have to be fast and stressful."

"What does it have to be then?" I grumbled.

"Just us," he murmured.

I sighed. "I don't even know what *us* is." This was all moving so fast. "Last night you had your tongue in my pussy, and today you're my doctor. Hell, it seemed like it was just last month you hated me, and this last week you've been charming, trying to win me over—"

"Is it working?"

A huff. "No."

Linc smiled, a slow curve of his lips that had my stomach clenching, my pussy throbbing as I remembered exactly how good it had felt to have his mouth there. "It's working," he said.

"It's not—"

His lips descended, dropping to mine and taking my mouth in a kiss that sent my pulse skyrocketing, my body drifting through space until it met the hard, glorious breadth of his.

"It's working," he said again. Then he released me, turned for the door. "I'll come by your rooms at seven."

He disappeared into a puff of smoke.

Okay, not so much smoke as the man silently walked

through the door and out into the hall, leaving me in the patient room with tingling lips, breath that still came in fits and gasps.

And a lady boner the size of a redwood.

This man was dangerous.

He was also right.

It *was* working.

———

I GLANCED AT MY WATCH, saw that it was 7:15, and made a face.

I shouldn't be disappointed.

I was the one who'd left my rooms at 6:30 with the express purpose of hiding from Linc.

Immature? Yes. Cowardly? Also yes.

Ridiculous in a small base where it wasn't that hard to find someone, especially with all the security measures in place? Triple yes.

But it was 7:15, and the man hadn't found me.

He was a KTS agent. He *should* have found my semi-lame hiding spot. The same semi-lame hiding spot that I was calling myself an idiot six ways to Sunday for using, and the same one I'd warred with myself for using.

It was just . . . I needed to keep something back.

Otherwise—

I was going to get hurt.

And yet, if I kept hiding, I was going to miss out. Seeing Dan and Ava, Laila and Ryker being so fucking happy was giving me serious FOMO vibes. What if Linc was my Dan, my Ryker? What if we could have what they had?

But . . . how could we?

Because I wasn't like Ava and Laila.

Yes, I hated myself for saying that. Yes, I knew I was pretty fucking great and smart. Yes, I knew that Linc was a good guy, had enough good guy examples in my life to recognize they weren't a rare species of unicorn. They existed. My friends were them. My friends *loved* them.

They existed.

The only niggling doubt was . . . did they exist for me?

And, yes, I hated myself for thinking that as well.

It was just . . .

What?

Easier to pretend I was lacking so I didn't have to take that step and put myself out there, didn't have to get burned again, to have my heart broken again? Yes. Because if I wasn't worthy, then I didn't need to let Linc close, and my armor stayed intact. See? The perfect scenario.

I stayed safe.

I continued doing a job I loved.

Except, FOMO.

Because if I fucking ran before I gave Linc and I a chance then . . . what?

I would be a fucking weakling, that was what.

I'd never run from a situation in my life. I'd paused, thought things through, made sure I was absolutely ready to commit. But then I jumped in with both feet.

And after spending the night in Linc's arms—and one day, too, I supposed—I needed to cut the wavering bullshit.

I'd already jumped.

To pretend otherwise was a waste of everyone's time.

I pushed out of the gym, where I'd been doing a pathetically small number of reps with a pathetically small amount of weight. "You are not a fucking coward, Olive. You get your fucking head straight and you fucking—"

"Distracted." A big body stepped in front of mine, making me skid to a stop. A large, gentle palm cupped my jaw. "Cursing."

I blinked up at Linc. "How the hell did you find me?"

"I pay—"

"Attention," I finished. Yes, my tone was a bit snarky. But

good God, did the man ever have another explanation? "What's the fucking truth?"

A shrug. "I followed you."

My eyes rose high enough to get lost in my hairline. "You *followed* me?" I glared, even though I was a bit embarrassed to not have noticed. Though, I supposed I already knew that Linc wouldn't hurt me, at least not physically, so perhaps my instincts had just accepted his presence without warning me.

Either that or I was really losing my touch.

"Yup." He slung an arm around my shoulder, tucked me against his side. "Got there at 6:30 because I knew you were going to try to pull a fast one. And unsurprisingly, you were just coming out of your room. It was easy to keep my distance and still keep track of you." He kissed the top of my head. "Figured I'd let you pump a little iron. Let out some of that frustration."

"*You're* the source of my frustration."

"I know." Another kiss to the top of my head had me squirming out of his arms. "Isn't it great?" he asked, reeling me back in and laying a hot, deep, wet one on me. No warning. Not moving slowly. No careful descent or overly gentle hands.

One moment we were several feet apart.

The next I was plastered against his chest, and his tongue was practically down my throat.

Or maybe that was *my* tongue down his? Maybe it was *me* pulling him closer instead of the other way around? I couldn't be sure, either way. And I supposed I didn't really care to find out, not when this man was kissing me like an absolute god, not when I was ready to tear both of our clothes off, right here in the hall.

Distantly, I heard a *click*.

Then voices.

But by then Linc's hand had moved to my butt, angling my hips against his erection, and fucking hell, that was good.

Good enough that I ignored whoever was coming our way.

"Holy balls."

Laila.

Fucking hell, my commanding officer had just stumbled across me sucking face with a fellow agent in a public area of a base. I tore my lips from Linc's, not really thinking as I wiped my mouth with the back of my hand, missing—or at least barely classifying the dark look that action rent on his face—and spun to face my boss.

Knowing my lips were swollen from said sucking face.

Knowing my cheeks were red-hot because holy hell, the man could kiss, and my C.O. was staring at me with amusement dancing across her face.

Knowing . . . that, *oh God*, I was never going to live this down.

"Lay," I said, swallowing hard several times until I could get some sort of statement out of my mouth. "Um. Hey. What's up?"

Some sort of statement being *not* a great one.

Laila cleared her throat, eyes filled with mirth. "Nothing much. What are *you* doing?" she asked innocently.

Nothing I hadn't caught her and Ryker doing a million times, and yet, *me* getting caught was critically embarrassing. Yet, me getting caught had me ready to commandeer some C-4 and blow a hole in the floor so that I could jump in it. And maybe use the rubble to bury myself.

"Nothing," I said, trying to play it cool. "I was just going to grab some dinner. Did you want to come with me?"

Her gaze flicked over my shoulder.

Linc was still at my back, his heat surrounding me, and I could have sworn I heard him curse . . . or maybe it was a growl?

Was it actually possible for a man to make that sound?

Regardless, he had. I heard it, felt it skid along my spine.

And Laila, apparently, heard it, too. Her lips twitched. "Not today, Ollie. I think . . . well, I think your dinner plans are already spoken for." She tugged a strand of my hair. "I'll catch up with you tomorrow, now that you're ready for some action."

"Light duty," Linc said.

Okay. *Growled.*

This time there was no swearing. It was definitely a growl. I spent a moment thinking about how that might feel between my thighs, only obliquely tuning into the conversation.

"What?" Laila asked.

"She's only cleared for light duty," he snapped, moving to stand in front of me, a position that had me focusing—and not on my fantasies involving this man. "Not action."

"Ah." Laila paused. "I would say this is *my* team, and I make the final determination for the members of it. However," she said, her tone turning teasing in a way that had me shoving at Linc's back, trying to move around him. "You've got the Ryker scowl happening, so I know that you've got all sorts of pesky emotions messing with your mind right now. Which means, I'll let your questioning of my decisions slide." Her voice hardened. "For this *one* time. Also, to put those *emotions* at ease"—here she patted him on the shoulder—"by *action,* I meant the copious amounts of files we need to go through in order to track down Daniel, since that's our mission now."

I finally succeeded in getting around Linc. "But what about the Mikhailova?"

"Back-burnered until we figure out the situation with Daniel."

I didn't like the idea of leaving the Mikhailova out there to potentially traffic and hurt more innocent people, but I understood that until we had taken out Daniel, KTS couldn't run effectively. How could we focus on taking out the bad guys if we had to spend most of our time watching our backs?

It wouldn't work.

But I still hated that the mob was out there, spreading their special brand of evil.

Still, I nodded and said, "Got it." Both because I did and

because Laila was my team leader, and this wasn't a moment to question her decision.

Her eyes flicked to mine then back over my shoulder again, mouth curving into a smile I couldn't begin to interpret. "Have fun, kids." She walked away. "Oh, and Ollie?"

I was frowning, trying to decode that smirk of hers. "Hmm?"

"Good luck with that."

"What?" My brows drew together, and I turned to glance up at Linc. "Why did she say good luck—"

His lips slammed down on mine.

This was heat and desire, but there was also a tinge of irritation laced in the contact, as though he were trying to brand me with his mouth, to imprint himself on my soul.

When we broke apart, my heart racing, it was to find that his gray eyes were filled with thunderclouds.

"Don't wipe that one off," he muttered, taking my hand and tugging me forward.

My chest was heaving in a way that spoke very little to the copious amounts of cardio I forced myself to do. "What are you talking about?"

He leaned down, nipped my bottom lip. "You wiped your mouth earlier, like you were ashamed, like you were dirty after my kiss."

I thought back, confusion warring with irritation. "That's not what I was doing."

A brow lifting. "Then what *were* you doing?"

"I don't know," I said, shrugging. "I just . . . wasn't thinking, I guess. Laila caught us, and I was—"

"Ashamed?" The question was deathly quiet.

"No," I said quickly. "I was just . . . embarrassed, I guess. I'm not used to people coming across me when I'm . . ."

"Sticking your tongue down someone's throat?"

I winced. "Yeah. That."

His lips pressed flat, and I finally noticed what was behind the irritation in his gaze. There was hurt in those storm-cloud gray eyes, and it made my heart squeeze. Because I could see a slender thread of insecurity, and I didn't want him to feel that way, to think I was ashamed of him, ashamed of what we were doing.

I *couldn't* let him think that.

I stepped closer, wrapped my arms around his waist. "Do you know what I was planning on doing when I came out of the gym?"

"No," he grumbled.

"I was planning on coming to find you," I said. "Because all day long, I could only think of the ways this could go wrong. How I could get hurt, how you would prove to be like every other jerkwad I'd ever dated." He scowled, and I hurried to add, "But as I was sitting there thinking of all the things that *could* go wrong, thinking that I needed to get the hell out before I was in too deep, I realized I was *already* in deep." I cupped his cheek. "For better or worse, I like you, Linc. I like you a whole hell of a lot, and I was kidding myself in thinking that I didn't want this, that I could possibly be happy if I didn't give it a chance." My lips found his for a brief kiss. "I want you. I want to find out what this is between us. Because"—and here I had to push past the fear that wanted to sink its talons in and shake me firmly until I'd regained my normal caution—"I think this thing between us might run deep."

He didn't move.

For an eternity, he didn't move.

His eyes were wide and locked on mine, his lips flattened out, his jaw clenched, a muscle ticking along one side.

"Fuck, baby." And then he was lifting me up, turning to pin me against the wall. "Yes, this runs deep," he said. "This runs really fucking deep."

And then he kissed me again.

And I found I didn't care who might stumble upon us.

Because Linc had me covered.

CHAPTER TWELVE

KTS Satellite Base
Western Georgia
7:22hrs

Linc

I REALLY WAS NOT happy to be crawling out of bed, leaving a softly snoring Olive behind, her hands pillowed beneath her, her expression placid, her body clad in the cutest fucking pajamas I had ever seen.

Tiny sheep playing guitars. A matching bright blue tank top with—kill me now—no bra.

I wanted to go back to bed, to curl up next to her.

It had been ten days since the accident, and that meant my mental timer of how long I'd promised myself I wouldn't touch her had run out. Yes, I'd failed on the touching part, but also, since I'd really meant touching her with my penis—that throbbing fucker had been angrily cooped up for the entire time in her presence over said ten days—I'd consider it a partial success.

I hadn't fucked her.

She was on light duty, ten days recovered, so could we . . . lightly fuck?

Stifling a groan, I softly tiptoed out of my room and headed into the hall. I would be off base all day on a reconnaissance mission with my team. Hannah had issued a call time of 7:30. Which meant she'd really issued a time of 7:15.

So, technically, I was already late.

Not that I begrudged myself the extra few minutes with Olive. It was almost frightening how fucking perfect it felt to hold her in my arms, to be able to talk and lie with her, and now that her team was based out of the Georgia compound during her, Ava's, and Dan's recoveries, I would have that opportunity for a while.

The next step—planning for what would come when she returned to England, since my team's current mission was based in the States—was a concern in the back of my mind for a bit, rather than something I worried about every second of every day.

Plot and plan.

Figure out all possibilities.

Then worry.

Or hopefully, *not* worry because everything between us would sort itself out.

"You going to stand there all day staring dopily at the wall?" Hannah asked, pushing open the door next to the expanse of said wall outside the staging room that I *had* been staring at quite dopily. "Or are you going to come through, so we can get our asses in gear?"

I scowled. "The second one."

"Does this dopey state have anything to do with one sexy doctor?" Lily asked.

I rolled my eyes.

"It does. Ha!" She put her hand out to Jesse, the final member of our team. A broad-shouldered redhead with a killer hand at explosives, she was the absolute shit, and we were lucky to have her. "Pay up," Lily said. "You owe me twenty."

"Lily," I warned.

"Hey, don't look at me. Jesse here"—a twenty was smacked into her palm by an irritated-looking Jesse—"*she's* the one who bet against you. I, for one, would never bet against the good doctor with the dreamy eyes and the body like"—a chef's kiss—"a fine wine with a plate of steaming rigatoni Bolognese."

Lily, outside of the operating room and in the field (where she was kickass at both), was best taken in small doses.

Especially, when she had a bee in her bonnet. Like, apparently, today.

"Enough," Hannah said. "It doesn't matter what Linc does with his personal time." Her lips tipped up at the edges, and I knew I wouldn't be spared her quiet brand of teasing. "Even if that personal time *does* involve the sexy doctor we prefer."

"I feel like I should be offended," I muttered, strapping a knife to my thigh.

Hannah tightened her ponytail before starting to check her equipment. "Oh, don't get offended. It's only because Lily and I would totally do her—that is, if she was into women in the least. It has nothing to do with you and your yummy abs."

I scowled again.

"The worst part," Lily grumbled, "is that I asked her out once."

"What?" I whirled to face her, eyes narrowing.

Lily fluttered hers back in my direction. "Oh, *stop* with the caveman-she's-mine-bullshit," she said. "It was way before this thing you two have—which, by the way, is a thing with enough sparking chemistry to light a fucking room on fire, and also something that means no one else in their right mind at KTS would dare to make a show of interest." A beat. "For *either* of you—"

I frowned, glanced to Hannah, who nodded in agreement, and felt relief slide through me.

Probably, that made me an asshole.

But I was an asshole who didn't care, because I'd just squeaked out a second chance with Olive, and I didn't want anything to get in the way of it.

"What happened when you asked her out?" Jesse probed as she shouldered her pack.

Lily buckled the front of hers. "Well, I asked her on a date not long after she'd been recruited, and let's just say, she turned me down, albeit very gently and nicely, but in a way that made it clear she was strictly heterosexual."

That made a bolt of guilt stab straight into my heart.

Because I hadn't turned her down nicely. Or gently. And yup, fuck, I *was* an asshole.

An asshole trying to make up for what I'd done, but an asshole, nonetheless.

"That sounds like her," Hannah agreed. "She's really nice."

"Yup." Jack clapped me on the back. "And too nice for the likes of you, that's for damned sure."

Jesse laughed as she headed for the door. "She sure is. You'd better play your cards right, so she doesn't figure out that she's way out of your league."

"Hilarious," I muttered, shrugging into my own pack. "Gotta love teammates that have your back."

"Oh," Lily said. "We have your back." A shrug. "It just doesn't mean I have to kiss your ass."

"Again. More hilarity."

Lily chuckled as she followed Jesse out the door, Jack following suit in his much more typically quiet manner. That quiet meant he was a major asset for the gossiping old nags on base. He had the ability to be so still, to melt into the shadows so effectively that people forgot he was there.

And then they spilled their guts.

And *then* those guts were painted all over this base . . . and the ones abroad.

Not the prettiest imagery, but then again, I *was* a doctor.

"Chin up, Linc," Hannah said, plunking my hat onto my head. "It's not so bad."

"For you." More muttering as I straightened the hat she set there, tugging it out of my eyes. Pretty soon I was going to be turning into a teenager. Good times.

"Meh," she said. "You'll survive." She bumped her shoulder to mine. "Plus, I like Olive for you. She's wonderful and will treat you right, *and* she won't take any shit." A beat as she studied my face, expression going uncharacteristically serious. "But more importantly, you deserve someone to treat you right."

That much was true.

The shit-taking part, anyway. The rest of it . . . well, there *was* a reason my ex had cheated, and it wasn't just because I was always traveling for work.

"Linc."

I glanced up.

"You're good for her, too, you know?"

I nodded, even though deep down, I couldn't deny that the notion gave me some pause. Was I really?

Not that I had time to ruminate on that lovely thought.

I needed to get my head in the game, get ready for the mission we were about to head out on. I needed to plan and plot and focus . . . because I didn't want to end up dead.

I *wanted* to end the night back in Olive's arms.

Especially since it was day ten.

———

UNFORTUNATELY, I *didn't* end up back in Olive's arms.

I didn't get to celebrate day ten.

Instead, I first sweated my ass off during the hot-as-hell fall Georgian day, and then froze my ass off during the chilly fall Georgian night, spending hours watching a shitty house on the edge of town.

The target we had been tracking hadn't shown at the time our informant had specified, and we had been in the process of leaving some surveillance equipment in order to catch a glimpse of him before heading back to the base when the fucker had appeared.

Then had *stayed*.

And had been a markedly stupid criminal.

Turned out, the dumbass had stolen nearly a million dollars' worth of opioids and had been pursued by the dealer he'd taken the load from. Which meant that we stumbled onto the man we'd been working for months to take down.

It had all just happened in a way that was totally fly-by-the-seat-of-our-pants and riding that line between FUBAR and we might just scrape this one out.

In the end, we'd gotten our target, the dealer, and five of the guys, but we had to wait until nearly dawn for reinforcements from headquarters and for the dumbasses to drink themselves into a stupor with alcohol provided to them by the man who'd stolen the goods.

Thankfully, the rotgut had made the dealer and his cronies slow, otherwise the firefight might have turned out very different.

But other than a twisted ankle—Lily had missed spotting some sort of critter's burrow when we were laying down cover fire—and a bullet graze on Ryker's arm— he hadn't dodged in time to avoid the furrow on his biceps—everyone had come out unscathed and satisfied with our takedown. Luckily for my team, Ryker and Laila had been able to come in to support when we realized we'd needed backup for the takedown.

A takedown the local police would get the credit for.

But we'd get the dealer—she would be going into custody at KTS.

And, for the moment, the world was a better place.

But right now, exhaustion making my limbs heavy, my eyes absolutely burning from the lack of sleep, I didn't give a shit about the world. I wanted to shower then go find a place to sleep, preferably that place being in Olive's bed.

I dropped my gear back in the staging room and headed for my quarters, knowing that even though I wanted to find my Pop, I wouldn't interrupt her rest.

And I was feeling very surly about what would soon be my rest in my empty and cold-ass bed.

Which was why I didn't see it.

Or *her* rather.

She pushed out of the shadows and launched herself into my arms. "Are you okay?"

"Olive?" I asked dumbly, since she was quite literally in my arms.

One look at my face had her stepping back. "What's wrong?"

I shook my head. "Nothing," I said. "You just surprised me."

"That"—a wave of her hand in the direction of my face—"is not surprise, and neither was it surprise giving you that dark look a few moments ago. What's going on? Is someone hurt?"

"No, aside from a twisted ankle and a bullet graze, everyone's fine."

She breathed out a relieved sigh. "Then what is it?"

"Nothing." I took her hand, my heart fucking hammering in my chest. My legs were shaky. Because it *was* something all right. It was something huge and soul-shattering because . . . she was there. "I just need a shower and some sleep." There. My tone sounded normal. Sort of. "Let's go back to my place."

It was just . . . Olive was there.

I didn't realize until that moment how much I'd expected it to be the opposite.

But she *was* there, waiting for me. Happy to see me, concerned for me. Not angry or resentful or . . . ready to strike out like a pissed-off snake. Read: she hadn't reacted like my ex. Wasn't furious I hadn't made contact when the mission hadn't gone as planned. I supposed that was because Olive was an agent herself, so she knew what it was like—that things could change on a dime, plans could alter, and I might be gone for more than twenty-four hours instead of the planned eight.

But . . . it was more than that.

She was there, with her hand in mine, being fucking sweet and awesome.

And . . . I fell in love.

Or maybe I'd been there already. I'd certainly known that I'd wanted to keep her forever. Then add in her taking care of me by tugging me back to my room, warming up the shower, grabbing me fresh clothes—read: not like my ex—and . . .

I fell deeper.

I knew that no matter what happened, this woman would always hold my heart in the palm of her hand.

Just as I knew, it would always beat for her.

Only for her.

CHAPTER THIRTEEN

KTS Satellite Base
Western Georgia
9:46hrs

Olive

I HADN'T UNDERSTOOD it until then.

Well, until Linc strode back onto the base, tired in his eyes and weary in his expression. His team had been out of contact for more than a day—well, *Linc* had been out of contact with me for more than twenty-four hours. His team had coordinated a response with Laila and Ryker and another team on base in order to bring the right amount of firepower to a situation that was going to go down, and go down hard.

So, I'd known where Linc was, where Laila and Ryker were, but I couldn't do a damned thing about it.

And for a woman who was used to being on the front lines, I hadn't liked that.

At all.

But it was the job, and sometimes the job meant that missions went south, and people got hurt. I had worried about

Linc (and Laila and Ryker and everyone else out there), but I had tried not to. I knew they'd be as safe as possible.

Still, it had been an odd situation.

Normally, I would have been in the field, been able to know every bit of information they had. So this whole waiting around, twiddling my thumbs, while trying to bury that discomfort, the agony of being on the sidelines, all while hoping to hear news was not for the faint of heart.

NOPE. No way.

Then he'd walked in, and I'd realized Linc had expected one of two things. One, for me not to be waiting for him to return to base, and two, if, by chance, I *had* been waiting, he'd been braced for my anger.

And that hurt my heart.

He'd been prepared for either vitriol or absence, and I fucking hated that he'd anticipated being on the receiving end of either.

Linc was sweet, funny, and annoying in equal turns—cue inner snort. But the point was that he was a good guy, and aside from that one supremely jerky moment during which he'd hurt my feelings a few months back and for which he'd apologized, he'd treated me with kindness and respect.

Did we butt heads?

Heck yes.

Did he never miss a moment to call me on my shit?

Also, yes.

But was he one of the smartest, sexiest, loveliest men I knew?

Yup.

So, that's why it killed me that he'd expected to get shit on after a long fucking night, after a long fucking day, both of which meant that he and the other agents had to be running on fumes of adrenaline because their careful planning had been turned on its head.

"Fucking motherfucker," I murmured. I wanted to find out where his ex lived and go over to throttle her.

"Distracted."

I blinked, took in the yummy picture that was Linc emerging from the bathroom in a cloud of steam, just a towel around his waist, and his yummy chest and abs on display. "What the hell are you talking about?"

"You're distracted," he murmured, running a finger down my throat. I was in a simple hoodie and sweats that weren't see-through this time around. A fact I was absolutely certain of because I'd played all sorts of acrobatics—acrobatics that would certainly make him furious if he'd seen me attempt them—in front of the mirror in my quarters, ensuring that no amount of squatting, bending, or material pulling taut would reveal my bright blue hedgehog-printed undies.

"I'm not fucking distracted."

Lie.

I'd *been* distracted before.

I was even *more* distracted now. His stubble had transformed into a full beard, and water droplets glistened in the dark brown hairs. My mind was completely focused on that beard and wanting said beard between my thighs again, feeling those cool droplets against my skin, mixing with the heat of his mouth as he kissed his way up my legs.

Nope.

I wanted that beard, that mouth against my pussy.

But he'd had a long night, and before I'd gotten distracted by the whole beard, shirtless, precariously perched towel situation, I'd been heading out to get him food. He needed a good meal, and he needed sleep.

He *didn't* need me jumping him like he was a tree and I was the cat desperate to climb it—or rather, *him*.

Linc stepped close. *Real* close.

My breath caught. My pulse pattered like a machine gun, a rapid *thrum-thrum-thrum-thrum-thrum-thrum.*

The slightly damp heat of his chest was soaking through the cotton of my hoodie, the fabric of his T-shirt I wore beneath it. The one I'd swiped from his hamper to sleep in the night before when he hadn't come back to base because the annoying man had gotten me addicted to sleeping in his arms, his scent covering me, his gorgeous body wrapped around mine.

"Hey, Distracted, what are you thinking?" He ran his knuckles down my throat, making me shiver, making the words in my throat unstick.

"I stole your fucking shirt," I blurted.

He pulled back slightly, surprise in his gray eyes, but his lips were curving, tipping up at the edges, and then his hand cupped my cheek. "You stole my shirt?"

Heat singing my cheeks, I nodded.

"Why, baby?"

Clearing my throat, I asked, "Why what?" I knew what. *Of course,* I knew what. I just . . . didn't know if I could put myself out there that far yet.

But then I thought of the look on his face when he'd seen me in the hall, and I knew that I *had* to put myself out there. At least a little bit. Because this man deserved it, and also because I deserved to have something that was honest and meant something. We both deserved to have something big, something that blew the roof off this freaking building, right?

A mental nod.

Damn right, we did.

"You weren't here," I whispered, hating that his expression clouded, and so I quickly added, my fingers stroking over the rough bristles on his jaw, "So I found a way to sleep with you around me."

His lips parted.

His eyes darkened. *"Pop."*

"Why do you call me that?"

"You slept in my shirt?"

My cheeks grew even hotter.

"Baby?" he pressed, his hand brushing over my throat, back and forth, back and forth, lifting the hairs on my arms, making a shiver skate down my spine.

And cue more blurting. "I still have it on."

Another slow, sexy smile, those fingers coming to the hem of my hoodie, slipping beneath the material of his shirt to stroke across my abdomen. "You do?"

I nodded.

"Why?"

"It's early." A beat. "I didn't have time to change."

His other hand came up, tugged a lock of my hair. "No, that's not why."

I sighed, wrinkled my nose. "Why doesn't matter." I lifted my chin. "Except the why for *why* you call me *Pop*."

"I call you *Pop* because you're Olive, like Olive Oyl."

My nose stayed wrinkled. "You've been calling me *Pop* because of *Popeye?*"

Yuck.

He laughed, stroked a finger down my nose. "Yes."

Well, way less romantic than I'd been expecting. I mean . . . Popeye was fine, I supposed. He just wasn't a character I was particularly excited to being compared to. "That's—"

"Not what you think."

"Except," I muttered, "it *is* like I think because you're comparing me to a bicep-bulging, spinach-eating sailor."

Linc's fingers drifting lightly across my skin. "Popeye's strong."

I raised my brows.

"*You're* strong."

I waited for more of an explanation. "That's it?"

His lips twitched. "That's it."

I swatted him on the chest, or at least I'd intended to. But then my hand made contact with his skin and instead of being a swat, it became a caress.

No, a *cup*.

Of those glorious pecs and then my other hand joined the first, and all of a sudden, I had two fucking incredible handfuls, and I suddenly didn't care that this man thought I was a bulky sailor.

Running his hand over my hair, he murmured, "It's not supposed to be an insult, baby. It's just what I thought of the moment you introduced yourself." He paused, met my eyes. "You walked in with tight jeans snug on your ass, combat boots on your feet, a smile as bright as sunshine on your face. And I discounted you. I thought, how in the fuck can a woman this sweet be at KTS?"

One half of his mouth curved. "But then you called me on my shit approximately one-point-two seconds into our conversation—and called me on it rightly. I was wrong. You were correct, and you were the first damned person in a really long time to have done that."

He wove his fingers into my hair. "And you did it all with that smile, did it all sweet. Then when I pushed back, when my ego got in the way and I questioned you—even knowing that you were right—you showed me spine. You showed me strength." He brushed his lips to mine. "You were Popeye, not Olive."

I inhaled sharply, more touched than I probably should be with just a silly nickname, but . . . I was still touched.

Even more so when he said, "If it bothers you, I'll stop. I promise."

My hands were still involved with their cupping, with the sweet words and silly nickname that was making my heart go all fluttery, and as thus, it took a moment for me to process what he'd said.

What he'd offered.

God, he was just so freaking *nice*.

"I was going to get you some food," I whispered, tilting my head toward the door.

His eyes went soft. "I'm not hungry, baby," he murmured, still stroking my hair. "We grabbed some junk food on the way back to base."

My teeth found my bottom lip, nibbled lightly. "I . . . *um* . . . I also don't mind Pop." Not when he'd explained it like he had. "Though I do wish you'd give Olive some credit"—I lightly dug in my nails, found my banter—"with a little more screen time, I'm sure she could have saved Popeye instead of playing the damsel in distress."

"Ah, misogyny," he said lightly. "It's alive and well."

"I would like to think that a cartoon like that probably wouldn't be as successful in this day and age."

A chuckle. "I'd like to think you're right." A beat, the hand in my hair growing a little tighter. "You were going to bring me food?" He'd moved closer, so the question was a warm puff of air against my mouth.

I nodded, heat trickling down my torso, gathering between my thighs, making my breathing unsteady. My tongue darted out to find my bottom lip again. "Feed you," I whispered, ticking the items off on my fingers. "Tuck you into bed." Another tick. "Let you sleep."

His hand at my waist slid higher, dragging me a little closer. But I hardly noticed the loss in dexterity. Because all I could feel was Linc. "So, we can skip the first"—his hand moved higher—"forget the third"—higher—"and go straight to the second?"

"The second—" My question cut off as he began towing me toward the bed. "What are—?" He tugged the zipper of my hoodie down, nudged the fluffy cotton off my shoulders. "I can't—" It hit the floor with a soft *floof*. "I have to work."

He didn't answer, just stared at me.

"Linc?" I repeated. "I have to work."

"God, I love it when you wear my shirts," he growled, his mouth dropping to my jaw, dragging back toward my ear.

"You've—*ah*"—he nipped the lobe, making me shiver —"seen me in them before."

"Yup." Another nip. "I still love you in them."

"And—*eek!*" I found myself on my back on the mattress, a very strong and not sleepy *and*—it had to be said—precariously-towel-clad man on top of me. Who was staring down at me like he'd worked a long fucking night, and I was the last donut in the infirmary's staff room.

Just to be clear. I was the donut in this scenario.

And considering the heated, sexy-as-shit look in his eyes, the hand that was still moving on my skin, the mouth that was coming closer . . . I really didn't mind being the donut.

I'd be a chocolate glazed.

Or maybe a rainbow sprinkles.

Because I always loved color, and I like the idea of being the type of colorful this man devoured.

Devoured. Such a delicious word.

Such a delicious *feeling*, having this man want me.

"I made you squeak." His palm stroked higher, tracing the band of my bra.

"No—" My denial was interrupted even before I got it all the way out.

"It's been ten days."

I blinked at the sharp left turn in conversation. "Okaaay?"

He nipped at my bottom lip. "You're supposed to ask, 'Since *what?*'"

"Since what?" I parroted, my mouth twitching.

"Since you were hurt."

My brows drew together. "Actually, it's been elev—"

"Eleven. Right." He did some cupping of his own, first the left breast, then the right, and my nipples hardened against the fabric of my bra. I wanted the bra gone. I wanted the shirt gone.

I wanted my sweats and my cute hedgehog undies gone.

But mostly . . . I wanted this man.

"Linc?"

"Hmm?" His mouth dragged down my throat, tugging the loose neckline to the side, trailing his tongue along my collarbone.

"Are you saying your self-imposed vow of chastity is now over, and we can finally fuck?"

Gray eyes flying to mine. A heavy body above mine going so, *so* still.

A hard cock growing harder between my thighs.

I reached for the towel.

And that seemed to finally unfreeze him, to send him into a flurry of movement, of rapidly moving hands and shifting body parts, and . . . suddenly I was stripped down to nothing but my hedgehog panties and my boring white sports bra.

Linc's eyes were on my body—a long, slow stare that left my nerves on fire and had my thighs clenching around his waist. But he didn't move any farther, just stared.

I found myself getting tetchy.

"If you'd wanted some of that lace from your peeping Tom fantasies, you should have taken me on a date," I said, lifting my chin and crossing my arms over my chest. "Or maybe, more accurately, you should take me on that date you keep saying you're going to take me on."

A ghost of a smile. "I didn't say I wanted lace."

My brows lifted. "You don't?"

"I'm not opposed to it." He bent, kissed one globe of my breast then the other over the top of my sports bra. "I just am not saying I expected it." One flick and he nudged the band up, making my breasts pop free, kissing his way toward one nipple, stopping just before he sucked it into my mouth. "You want to wear lace, Pop," he said, lifting his head and meeting my eyes. "Then wear lace. You want to cover that sexy ass of yours in the biggest, ugliest pair of granny panties I've ever laid eyes on, great. I don't care. Because I would want you in a fucking garbage bag, in a chastity belt—" A shake of his head. "Okay, *not* the chastity belt because that would make what we're going to do next very difficult, but baby, I mean it when I say I fucking love you in sweats, I love you in those jeans with the torn right knee, I love you in hoodies, and I love you in my T-shirts. Wear what makes you happy, just so long as you let me take it off you."

Laughter bubbled up in my chest, and I shook my head. This man was just . . .

"God, I love when you laugh."

"Because you—" I broke off, a moan tumbling from my lips when he sucked my nipple deeply into his mouth.

"Because I what?" he asked after he'd released it with a soft *pop*. His fingers trailed over my abdomen, down toward my pussy in slow, steady circles. I could feel his erection poking into my thigh, and it was driving me to the edge of reason. Linc wanted me just as much as I wanted him, and yet, the blasted man kept stopping to have conversations with me.

Although, I kept having them, too.

Although, I could solve that problem.

But first . . .

"You like me laughing because it makes my tits jiggle." I waved a hand along my front. "Now, will you just get on with it?"

"Get on with what?" he asked innocently, brows up.

And that was the moment I decided I'd had enough talking, enough banter, enough teasing and gentle stroking.

I'd wanted this man for-fucking-ever, and I'd waited long enough.

I shifted my weight, lurched up and over in a move that was definitely not light duty, but one that also didn't make my healed injury hurt . . . all that much anyway. Regardless of the pinch of pain in my side, I had a really good reward at the end of it: Linc sprawled out beneath me.

"Get on with *this*," I murmured, dropping my mouth to his.

CHAPTER FOURTEEN

KTS Satellite Base
Western Georgia
10:08hrs

Linc

SHE KISSED me like I was her life's blood, like she couldn't get enough of my mouth, my tongue, my body.

And that was fine with me. On a normal day.

On a *normal* day, I'd let her take all the time in the world. To kiss me for an eternity, to sip at my mouth, stroke her tongue along mine, to tease me until I couldn't see straight.

But this wasn't a normal day.

It was Day Eleven.

And it was Eleven after ninety-six days of calling myself a dumbass, after eleven hundred and seventy-two days of finding her incredibly sexy—though knowing I was married and couldn't appreciate the sexy in any way, shape, or form. I had waited a long time for this.

And so had she.

So no, I couldn't let her take the lead, to break my control, to make this something fast and quick and *over*.

I *wanted* that.

Fuck, how I wanted that.

But she deserved better.

One rapid movement had her back beneath me. Her cheeks were rosy, the blue of her eyes darkened with desire, and her lips damp from our kisses. Quite simply, she was the most beautiful thing I'd ever seen.

But when I went to kiss her again, she stopped me, one finger pressing to my mouth.

"Lose that towel."

That was easy. It wasn't even hitched on my hips, more tangled around my thighs from all our flipping. A lift of my pelvis, one sharp tug, and it was gone, tossed over my shoulder to hit the floor somewhere behind me.

"You lose your clothes, too," I said, even though she was already tugging her bra over her head. I reached for the cute as fuck underwear and slid them down her thighs. Getting naked was probably a terrible idea—well, no. It was clearly the best idea we'd ever had. But it was also not great for my already fractured control.

When she was naked, I found I didn't give two shits about control.

I just needed to touch and kiss and stroke, and I needed to do all of that to every inch of her body, all at the same time.

What a moment to be a man and not an octopus.

Also, for the record, behind brokering world peace and curing child hunger, Olive's breasts definitely belonged on the list of things I wanted most. My mouth watered. My fingers itched. My cock—

"Linc?"

"Yeah, baby."

Her mouth twitched. "You can touch me."

A groan bubbled up in the back of my throat. "Yeah," I growled. "I want to do that."

And so I did.

Just like I'd imagined for so long. Running my palms over her torso, grazing them over her nipples, her rib cage, her navel. And everywhere my hands went, my mouth followed.

Her skin tasted like honey and strawberries with the barest hint of salt. Her hitching breath when I found a particularly good spot made my own lungs work like I'd run a marathon. Red had begun to edge into my vision, narrowing my focus to this woman, to wringing every bit of pleasure out of her.

With my fingers.

With my tongue.

Those breasts got attention—long draws and light strokes of my tongue, sharp nips soothed by a gentle mouth. I spent more time on her breasts than I ever did thinking about how I was going to broker that world peace or solve childhood hunger.

And then I kissed my way down between her thighs.

A firm caress through the damp heat of her, my mouth latching onto the bundle of nerves at the apex, finding it impossible to go slow. My cock was a throbbing beat in my groin, demanding I plunge home, that I take us both right over the edge. But the vestiges of my control reminded me that she needed to go first. She needed more.

Deserved *more.*

So . . . she got more. She got everything I had to give.

She got fingers sliding home, curling up to the angle she preferred. She got my tongue and teeth and lips working in tandem. She got to fly over that edge first, and without me.

But I didn't let up.

I knew she was sensitive, but I was too close to exploding.

If I slid home, I wouldn't last long.

And that meant she needed to be brought right back up to the precipice.

So my teeth and tongue and lips went back to work, leaving her clit alone until her hips started rocking against me again, until her head began thrashing on the pillow, until her legs opened wider, and I couldn't resist the siren's call of being inside her any longer.

One abrupt movement toward my nightstand, scrabbling through the drawer until I managed to pull out a condom.

Shaking fingers to roll it down the length of my cock.

Then I was back between her thighs, staring down at the woman I loved, knowing this was going to change everything.

For the better.

Slowly, I pushed in.

Slowly because even though it was day Eleven, I still needed to be careful.

Slowly because I wanted to savor this moment, wanted to remember how she felt the very first time I had her.

Slowly because the moment halted, inched forward, until we were reduced to two souls existing in one plane, one body, one perfect fraction of time.

And then I was in deep. Then her eyes were on mine.

Then . . . her hand lifted to cup my cheek.

And fuck if my throat didn't grow tight.

"Linc," she murmured.

"Yeah, baby?" I rasped out.

Intense blue eyes crinkled at the corners. "You can move now."

I did, but perhaps not in the way she intended. Because instead of pouncing on her like she was probably expecting, I peeled her hand off my cheek and laced our fingers together, resting our linked hands lightly on her chest, just above her heart, feeling it pound.

Her lips parted.

I kissed them.

Because I could.

Because I wanted to taste her moans when I started moving.

And finally, I did start moving, pulling out, pressing back in, slow and steady, finding a rhythm she liked, and then exploiting it until her moans were tumbling from her mouth to my own, until she broke her lips from mine, her head falling back to the pillow and her eyes squeezing shut.

I slowed, ignoring her when she protested. "No, baby," I said and waited.

She opened her lids, glared at me.

"Look at me when you come," I ordered.

Her gaze went hot. Her free hand gripped my hair, and she yanked my head down toward hers. "Don't stop, and maybe I *will* come."

I kissed her, hard and fast.

Then I started moving again.

And I didn't stop.

And then . . . she did keep those gorgeous blue eyes on me as she came, her pussy tightening around my cock, making me lose any semblance of slow and easy, making me forget she was injured as I thrust several more times before exploding.

Making me forget anything except that this woman was fucking perfect.

And that she was mine.

Would be mine forever.

———

WE WERE NECK-DEEP IN FILES.

And not a single one of them was making any bit of difference.

It had been forty-eight hours since we'd brought in our drug lord, and since there was nothing more to be done on that front for the moment, Hannah had decided our team's next mission would be to pool resources with Laila and Ryker and see if we couldn't get a lead on Daniel.

She'd framed it as Laila and Ryker needing help, since Ava and Daniel were still recuperating—Ava because KTS didn't have any magical broken-bone-healing agents (though I'd put it on my mental list of things to work on), Dan because he wasn't leaving Ava's side.

They'd stayed on base, since the location of Dan's house had been compromised in the same attack that had re-injured Ava's ankle and ended up getting Dan shot again, and for the most part, they'd sequestered themselves in their quarters.

This sequestering had been forced initially after Laila found out they were working on what had at first been called a vacation and later a convalescence.

She'd revoked their computer rights, confiscated their cell phones, and had locked them in their quarters. She'd even had their meals delivered.

So, on a whole, the locking in hadn't taken long to stick.

Because pretty soon, the new couple had been locking everyone *out.*

A fact Olive had told me with gleeful abandon just the night before, when we'd been doing some locking out of our own.

But none of that had anything to do with Ava's initial protests declaring she had a fucking broken ankle and wasn't a fucking invalid, mixing along with Dan's that he'd had the magic Ollie bandage and he was feeling absolutely fine. It didn't even have anything to do with the fact that they'd protested that Olive should be the one resting, and didn't she have vacation coming up?

Nope, instead, everyone had ignored them. Ava and Dan sequestering *was* overdue, and Olive should be resting (not that she would), and our team should be off doing something drug related.

That we weren't . . .

I knew it was because Hannah was doing me a solid.

Giving me more time with Olive.

And also stocking up on copious amounts of blackmail material for future dates.

But despite all of that—the sequestering, the gossip, the

complaining, me loving being with Olive—neither of our teams were any closer to locating Daniel.

He was a fucking ghost in the wind, and we didn't have a single clue as to where to find him.

No tracking on his old phone, no use of any of his old login credentials (not that they'd been valid since the moment he'd been kicked out of the squad, but we'd double-checked they hadn't been used anyway). There weren't any bank accounts in his name or any of the aliases we had on file. It wouldn't be hard for him to create another, of course, but the frustrating part was that . . . we just didn't have any leads.

Daniel had an ax to grind.

And that ax had nearly gotten my woman killed.

"Fuck," I muttered, tossing the file down and moving to the window of the conference room we were currently taking over. The bulletproof (and bomb-proof because I'd made damn sure of that after the incident in the garage) glass looked over the covered pavilion—a sheltered outdoor space that brought in much-needed sunlight without sacrificing security. Today there were a couple of teams on sight, most just shooting the shit, chilling in the daylight, enjoying the first non-humid day in months. One was clearly planning a mission, maps spread on a table, electronic tablets in hand as they plotted. Another group was practicing a type of sparring that took each of them to the thick grass planted along one side frequently and often.

But in here, we were going around in circles.

A warm hand slid around my waist, a head rested on my shoulder, flooding my nose with the scent of strawberries and Olive. "We'll find him," she murmured.

I nodded, knew I shouldn't be frustrated.

We'd just started on the case, and these things always took time.

But Daniel had hurt Olive.

Which meant the fucker had to pay, and the longer he was out there, the longer he had a chance to slip away.

"We don't even know if he did it," she murmured, her eyes on the glass, studying the scene.

"He fucking did it," I muttered, slipping my arm around her and drawing her closer. "We've checked everyone else who was on base that day, and they don't have motive, let alone had any opportunity." The cameras, the keycards, the access codes. All showed that area completely clean at that time. Which was even more infuriating. I shoved my hand through my hair. "I've got no clue how the fucker did it, but I know in my gut that he was responsible for it."

She was quiet for several moments. "I think so, too." A soft sigh. "But," she whispered so low that I had to strain to hear her. "Actually, I found something, and—"

Her eyes darted to the side, and she straightened.

"Wh—"

A tiny shake of her head had me cutting off the question.

"What are the lovebirds up to?"

I turned, saw that Jack had come up behind me.

"Fuck off," I muttered.

"You treat me so nicely," he grumbled but didn't show any sign of leaving. Instead, he turned his gaze to the windows and watched the people outside.

Olive lifted on tiptoe. "Later," she said under her breath, dropping back down and heading to the table where we'd spread the fucking files out. It was littered with coffee cups and dirty plates, along with her hoodie crumpled into a ball. Something she apparently did when she was thinking—along with resting her forehead on that crumple as she read over the files for the umpteenth time.

Now she grabbed her jacket . . . and a file.

Then with a meaningful look in my direction, she swept from the room.

CHAPTER FIFTEEN

Olive

I'D SPENT the entire day in my rooms trying to puzzle out what I had uncovered and also, not wanting to believe *what* I had discovered.

The niggling I'd had when I'd seen the file had grown.

And my horror and fury had grown right along with it.

Because . . . seriously, what the fuck?

There had been an error in the file, so minute I might not have even noticed it, if I hadn't just read the one from the day before the attack.

One word missing from the report on the security checks.

And then reappearing the next day in that same report, written by the same agent.

I'd spent these last hours going over every report that agent had ever issued on security measures—and there were a lot of them, since this agent was in charge of them at this satellite base —and I'd never found that word missing.

All measures were executed and processed as is standard.

Versus.

All measures were executed and processed as standard.

Two letters, one word, and my instincts had prickled. Fuck, it was such a small thing, could easily be a simple typo. Except . . . I knew Tom, knew that he was an agent who was better suited to staying on base, on overseeing these procedures because he was *rigid.*

The man had a routine, and he didn't like it to be deviated from.

Maybe one might say a bomb was a big freaking deviation.

But bomb or not, I still didn't think he would have diverged from his report standards. He was a man interested in details and perfections . . . and I hadn't found that missing word anywhere else.

Which meant my instincts had prickled.

I'd begun digging.

First, on the file with the typo, ensuring that the typo was also on the electronic version and not just the paper copy I had —it was. Then trying to confirm if anyone else had accessed it to try to edit it. But aside from the requests for paper printouts by Laila and tracing it as attachments through internal base emails of our team and Linc's, it appeared that no one else had gone in and changed anything.

So, I'd pulled those other reports by Tom.

And I'd gone firmly down the rabbit hole.

Tom had used the phrase *as is standard* in every report except the one from the day of the explosion, and I'd gone through well over a hundred and fifty of them.

I gathered the printouts I'd made, stacking them together so I could carry them easily. Then I went to visit Tom.

The base's security manager wasn't hard to find.

It wasn't yet six-thirty when he called it a day and went to the mess for dinner, so I found him in his office, typing away at his computer.

I knocked on the door and the bushy-eyebrowed, gray-haired agent glanced up at me and smiled. "Olive, hi," he said. "I'm sorry, I don't have time to chat. I need to finish this up."

"I know." I stepped into the office and closed the door behind me anyway. "But this is important."

Pale brown eyes met mine, and I saw regret pass through them when he realized I was going to disrupt his schedule. But he gamely soldiered on, pushing the keyboard tray in and asking, "Are you all right?"

My heart was pounding, my nerves firing and telling me I was right on the precipice of figuring this out, of discovering what in the fuck was going on. But instead of alluding to any of that, I just nodded and said, "I'm fine, Tom. All recovered, and I'm sorry to bother you." A small smile greeted my apology, and he waved me on. "I'll let you get back to your work, but I just needed your backup paper copy of your report from the day of the bombing."

He stilled. "Why?"

I held his eyes. "I can't tell you that yet," I said. "Not until I know."

He was silent for several moments then nodded and went to the file cabinet where I knew he kept a printout of every copy of every report he'd ever written. He flicked through the tabs quickly then stopped, reached inside and tugged out a stapled stack of papers. "How'd you know I kept these?"

I reached for it. "You told me once over coffee."

"Lunch or breakfast coffee?" he asked suspiciously.

"Breakfast," I said. "I'd come in from a long night, you were just getting started. Our paths crossed at cinnamon rolls."

His expression gentled. "I love Tuesdays."

Tuesdays were cinnamon roll days. "Me, too."

He started to hand me the file, paused, took the staples out and put the whole stack into the copy machine. "Just in case," he said, handing me the original and putting the duplicate back into the file cabinet. "You'll explain later?"

I nodded.

He sat down, pulled out the keyboard tray, his eyes going to his computer screen. "Need anything else?"

"No," I said, shaking my head. "Thanks."

"Go on then." Tom jutted his chin toward the door. "Leave me to it."

I left him to it.

And I went back to my rooms, still carrying the stacks of folders. I hurried inside, and I spread the two files out on the desk.

On the left, my copy from what Laila had pulled.

On the right, Tom's printout.

On the left, *as standard.*

On the right, *as is standard.*

"Shit," I whispered, sitting back in my chair as confirmation of what I'd already known, or at least, what some part of me had already known.

I opened up my laptop, began searching for who might have access to be able to alter the reports. Slowly, I was able to eliminate name after name—either they were out on active missions or not in the country or working at another KTS base.

Except one.

And then I began to dig deeper on that one name.

And what I found out made my blood chill then anger quickly well up to take its place.

Because it became clear that Daniel wasn't working alone.

He'd had help.

From another of our own.

I shot to my feet, knowing that I needed to tell Linc, to tell Laila, to tell Hannah. Leaving the files, I hurried to my door, swung it open—

And didn't see the blow coming.
A burst of pain, the floor rapidly rising up to meet my face.
Then nothing but black.

CHAPTER SIXTEEN

KTS Satellite Base
Western Georgia
19:46hrs

Linc

I KNOCKED AT Olive's door.

Quietly.

Because she'd missed meeting up with us at dinner, hadn't come back to the conference room, and I had assumed she was sleeping. She still needed her rest, even though she seemed determined to get back to full steam much sooner than I was comfortable with.

Of course, my instincts told me that she should be swathed in bubble wrap and then cosseted away like a precious possession, not getting healthy enough so she could go out on active missions again.

Go out and put her life at risk again.

But I told those instincts to fuck off.

I knew they were wrong, that she was a talented agent, and

she was fucking smart enough to take every precaution to keep herself safe. I knew that, and I wouldn't limit her. Because I also knew it had never even crossed her mind to limit me in that way. So even though my ego and my protective instincts hated her putting her life at risk, I got it.

She was a KTS agent.

The risks came with her.

And I had to accept that otherwise, our relationship would never work.

It was just . . . I also knew that sometimes being a KTS agent meant that our safety was put on a back burner because someone else needed saving.

That was the part that really scared me.

That was the part I had to accept anyway.

When she didn't answer, I knocked again, a little louder. And then when she didn't answer *that*, I used the code she'd given me to open the door and go inside.

Immediately, my blood froze in my veins, and I yanked my cell out of my pocket, calling Hannah. "Olive's rooms. Now." I hung up, next phoned Laila, repeating the same order, and then I cleared the room. It didn't take long. The bathroom. The bed. The closet. By the time I'd checked the only places a person could fit, Laila and Hannah were coming in behind me.

Then immediately stopping.

"Fuck," Laila said. "What happened?"

I shook my head. "I came"—a glance at the clock—"less than five minutes ago. She didn't answer my knock, so I used the code she'd given me to come in and found it like this."

This being . . . a fucking disaster.

Papers everywhere, the desk chair knocked on its side. Her laptop open on the floor, its screen cracked. Blankets torn from the bed, clothes all over the floor. There was no way someone hadn't heard the disturbance . . . but then again, the nearly soundproof walls had probably prevented that.

Had she called for help and no one heard her?

My heart lanced open.

"Fuck," I hissed.

Laila had done the same as me—checking the bathroom, the bed, the closet, and then coming back to stand by me.

"Pull up her tracker," I ordered.

Laila nodded and typed rapidly into her phone. All KTS agents had a tracker implanted in the inside of their arm. The tiny device was smaller than a grain of rice, and it provided the base with our location if we ever went missing while on mission. As far as I knew, no one had ever needed it to search while actually at KTS headquarters.

But if she were here, the chip would tell us where.

Laila kept typing, paused . . . then cursed. "It's not picking up a signal."

I grabbed the phone. "That's not possible."

Another curse, and she snatched it back, jabbing at the screen. "I know it's not possible." She held it up so I could stare at the display, at the error message telling me that, in fact, there was no signal to be found.

"Is it possible the walls in the base are blocking it?" Hannah asked.

I nodded. Maybe the concrete was fucking with the signal, especially since the trackers were only supposed to be used to keep eyes on agents when they were off base on missions.

"Maybe." She sighed, pocketed her cell. "We need to organize a search of the base."

"I'm on it," Hannah said, and I turned to see she was. She'd already picked up her phone, was sending the alert for our team to meet up at Olive's rooms—I felt it buzz through on my cell—and I listened to Laila do the same, including calling in Ava and Dan.

When I sent a questioning look, knowing they were off, she shrugged. "They would never forgive me if I didn't let them in on this."

"Right."

Less than five minutes later, Ava, Ryker, Dan, Lily, and Jesse had joined us, and together we mobilized the other agents on base to begin a search. I was just heading out with Hannah to check our quadrant when Jack ran in, breathless with wet hair. "Sorry," he said. "I was in the shower and missed the alert. What's going on?"

"I'll explain on the way," Hannah told him, and she did, giving him the important details as we joined our group and methodically searched the entire base.

"The trackers should work," Jack said as we moved. "We've upgraded the design after what happened in Italy"—how Ava had initially been hurt—"they should be broadcasting through anything."

I didn't want to think what *that* meant.

Would they still broadcast if Olive was de—

I shook my head.

Not the time to think about that.

We moved through our section, and thirty minutes later, every room had been cleared, and the agents congregated in the mess to debrief. No one had seen any sign of her. No blood. No struggle. No alarms set or notes left. It was like she'd just fucking vanished into thin air and knowing that something had happened to *her* rather than someone having just trashed her rooms when she wasn't in there had terror gripping me tightly and making it difficult for me to think.

I did my best to try to push that down, to make a mental checklist of what to do, how to find her.

And that had me heading back to her rooms.

There had to be a clue there, something we'd missed.

Laila followed me, and we both surveyed the mess of papers for a moment before diving in. "I'm guessing she found out how Daniel got the bomb in," Laila said, stepping forward.

She must have. Otherwise she would be here and not hurt or dead—

Not now.

Instead, I nodded. "She told me earlier that we'd talk later."

Laila's expression filled with determination. "We need to get a lock on her movements ASAP. Figure out what she discovered."

"I know."

Hannah appeared behind us. "I agree."

Ignoring them as they hashed out which agent was going to do what, I moved toward the desk, toward the scattering of papers and quickly snapped shots of the mess, just in case we needed them later. Then I began picking up file folders and printouts and began sorting through what Olive had been working on.

Laila helped while Hannah coordinated.

Then Dan found us and began helping, too.

Ava and Ryker had been ordered to scour the area surrounding the base for any sightings of her—hacking into the security systems of nearby gas stations, bus stops, train stations, airports and seeing if any cameras caught her, then set up back-doors into their systems that would alert us if Olive was moved. Hannah also mobilized Jesse and Lily to help track down Olive's pin and keycard so we could trace her movements from the day.

Jack, since he was our resident tech guy—he'd helped set up the security protocols that protected KTS's internal servers—had been given Olive's laptop and told to work on it and report back if he'd been able to recover anything.

"Got it," he said, taking it from Hannah. "I'll be in my lab if you need me."

Hannah nodded. "Roger that."

And I was left with . . . signs of a struggle, no blood—which made me only mildly less worried because a person could do a lot of damage without spilling blood—and aside from those two facts, I had nothing.

I knew Olive wouldn't disappear without telling me, without at the very least, telling *someone* or leaving a note.

She wasn't the type to run off half-cocked.

She was smart and deliberate, like I needed to be.

I blew out a breath and refocused.

Once Jack had left, Hannah came over and joined us to help stack the papers. "Let's bring these to the conference room," she suggested. "We'll have room to spread out and sort through everything."

Since that was logical, and I *really* needed logical right now, I just nodded, picked up what I could carry, letting the others get the rest, and hauled ass to the conference room we'd been working in. One movement of my arm shoved the materials we'd been studying earlier to the side (and most of them onto the floor, though I wasn't worried about that in the least). My next was to set the papers down, fingers and mind flying through them as I tried to sort them into some sort of order. It took Laila coming in on one side, Hannah on the other for them to make any sense, and then once we'd realized what she'd had —security reports from Tom—the process moved quickly. The files fell into proper stacks.

"Go talk to Tom," Laila ordered Dan, who'd joined in on the sorting.

He nodded, disappeared out of the room, and the rest of us kept working. Sorting the papers by date, scouring them all for anything. *Anything.*

And then I saw it.

The word *is* circled in red ink.

Just *is*.

"What the fuck?" I murmured.

"What?" Laila asked.

I showed her and Hannah, then flipped back through the rest of the papers in front of me. Nothing else was circled, and the word *is* appeared plenty of times throughout the reports.

"See if you can find page six in all these reports," I said, seeing the number on the bottom right.

She and Hannah didn't ask questions, just tore through the files and found any page six they could get their hands on. We shoved the others back, stacked those page sixes in front of us, searching for something that made sense. They all had the *is* circled, and further that, even though the *is* was found on different parts of the page, they were all part of the same sentence.

"They're all identical," I muttered, trying to figure out what in the ever-loving fuck Olive had been looking for.

"The same sentence," Laila agreed, her finger running over the page as she read.

I followed suit, skimming all of them, looking for anything other than the word *is* circled in the sentence, *All measures were executed and processed as is standard.* But that's all it was. One hundred and fifty-two page sixes, all with *is* circled, all surrounded by that same sentence, and not one other fucking clue on any of the papers.

There was a knock, and since it came at the point in this process when I was ready to tear my hair out, I shoved back from the table and went to the window, just barely resisting the urge to punch the fucking glass until I hurt, until I felt something other than this fucking panic that was twisting my insides into knots. I wanted to feel anything other than scared. I wanted to do something besides staring at goddamned papers. I wanted to make sure Olive was safe.

And I wanted to tell her that I loved her.

Because I hadn't had the chance yet.

Because I'd planned to tell her on the fucking date I hadn't yet taken her on, the one I'd plotted and arranged down to the minute, the one I'd promised myself would be so special and perfect that she wouldn't be able to tell me anything except she loved me right back.

But now, I was fucking terrified that I wouldn't get the

chance to take her on that date, to tell her that I loved every fucking inch of her.

"Linc."

Hannah put her hand on my back.

I resisted the urge to shake it off, knew that was just because I was feeling frustrated and worried and—God, those two words couldn't even begin to encapsulate exactly what I was feeling. They were too small. They were fucking shadows of the emotions tearing through my insides.

"Yeah?" I asked, turning slowly from the glass. It was too dark to see outside, and anyway, there wasn't anything to see—anyone who was on base was helping with the effort to locate Olive.

"You need to hear this," she said, and I followed her back to the table.

Tom had a file in hand.

He set it on the table. "She came just a few minutes before my dinner"—which meant just before 6:30, since Tom ate in the mess at that time every day like clockwork—"asked me if I had a paper copy of my security report. I did and gave it to her."

"What's that?" Laila asked.

"A copy of what I gave her." He shrugged. "I didn't want it to get lost"—Tom also didn't put a lot of faith in computers—"so I made an extra copy. She took the original." He glanced toward Linc. "Now she's gone, and I know it's got to be important."

Understanding finally dawning, I reached for the file.

"Be careful with it," Tom said. "I—that's my last one."

I nodded, flipped the pages carefully, stopping when I reached the sixth. Hannah and Laila once again sandwiched me, eyes scouring the page until—

"There!" Laila said, pointing at the sentence.

I read . . . and felt disappointment flood through me. It was the same. No *is* circled, of course, but the same sentence.

All measures were executed and processed as is standard.

"What does this mean, Pop?" I whispered. "What did you find?"

"What are you looking at?" Dan asked, bending over the table. I pointed. He frowned. "Wait." He straightened, began going through the papers again. "I thought I saw—yeah, *here*." He held up a page. "You guys missed one."

Laila snagged it, laid it next to Tom's report.

"Find the other," she ordered, and we scoured the stacks until we found the third page six that was from that date.

Tom stepped forward. "That's my copy." He tapped the upper left corner. "I print all of them on watermarked paper."

"Why?" Dan asked.

"I—"

"It doesn't matter," I snapped. "*Look.*"

Because I finally got it.

The copy Tom had just brought and the copy he'd given Olive earlier had watermarks. The third did not—which made sense because we'd printed these off and not Tom. What *didn't* make sense?

The fact that the copy *we'd* printed had no *is.*

"Find the rest of it," Hannah ordered.

We dove through the pages, Tom muttering something about organization, but we were beyond that by now. We knew we were close to the answer . . .

Then we had all the pages.

We arranged them in order, read them line by line, comparing them with the watermarked reports.

And still the only difference was the *is.*

"Fuck," I hissed, sinking into a chair, my head in my hands, my mind spinning, knowing we were missing something and so fucking frustrated that we couldn't figure out what it was.

Tom sighed, started lining the pages up in proper order. "I'll kill the bastard who fucked with my report. I work hard on making every sentence . . ."

He kept talking.

I stopped listening.

Because my eyes had gone to Hannah's.

"Fucked with the report?" she mouthed.

And suddenly, what Olive had been looking for finally became clear.

CHAPTER SEVENTEEN

Unknown location
Unknown hrs

Olive

I AWOKE SLOWLY, carefully taking stock of my body—my head throbbed, and my knee felt like it had been twisted the wrong way, but no other injuries were apparent in my prone position.

That prone position was with my hands bound in front of me and in some sort of moving vehicle.

I wasn't in a trunk—the material beneath me was too soft for that, but I also didn't think I was riding high in the back of a limo. Nope, it felt more like the back seat of a sedan, especially as I became more aware of my surroundings and my body and felt the buckle of a seat belt dig into my hip.

Ignoring that—because I couldn't risk moving and giving away any advantage of my being awake—I focused on the swaying of the car (gentle) and the noises outside (loud, as in we were moving fast).

Likely, I was on a highway.

The question was whether it was in a busy area where I might be able to evade whoever had kidnapped me from the base (and I had a fucking good suspicion of whom that might be) long enough to have a chance of finding a phone and calling in the big guns, or if it was in the middle of nowhere, and I needed to find a place to hide long enough for base to find my location via my tracker.

But . . . shouldn't they have found me already?

Hadn't anyone noticed I was missing at all?

I sure as hell hoped so, otherwise, my demise might be just around the corner.

"I know you're awake."

I stopped breathing.

Or not so much that, as I kept it slow and steady, even when another voice came closer and shoved hard at my injured side. Which fucking hurt. Just because the stitches were out and my namesake bandage was the shit at healing, didn't mean the area loved being poked and prodded.

But I bit back my cry of pain, held perfectly still.

"She's still out," the man who'd poked me said, and I felt the air shift as he sat back into the passenger's seat.

"I don't get why you grabbed her," the driver said. "You would have been better off killing her and then getting the fuck out."

"She knew," the passenger said. "She knew what I'd done. I needed to make sure she hadn't told anyone."

"What difference did it make?" the driver ask. "You were smoke anyway. She's a liability and—"

"She's mine," the passenger growled. "She was never supposed to get hurt in the first place. That bomb wasn't intended for her, and you know it. If you'd done your job correctly, she wouldn't have gotten hurt, and then I—" He broke off.

The driver chuckled. "You what? Would have had her?" He laughed harder. "Bro, she's never going to be interested in you.

That's not how Ms. Prim and Proper rolls. You're dirty, and she avoids the mud like it would give her the plague."

"She likes me," the passenger muttered.

"She likes *everyone.*"

"I could have convinced her to come along. To help us."

"*You* could have?" A moment passed. "No, dumbass, you couldn't ever have convinced her to join our cause. Ms. Prim and Proper doesn't have a traitorous bone in her body, and she's so in love with the agency that she wouldn't ever betray them."

That was true.

My parents had died when I was a child, leaving just my grandmother to raise me. Still, it wasn't the sad story it might seem. Yes, I'd lost my parents far too early, but my grandma had been wonderful. I'd felt loved and safe, and I'd never felt like I was missing out on anything. But it had just been the two of us for as long as I could remember. So when she had died, I hadn't had anyone.

When I was recruited, straight out of medical school, I'd had high test scores, a decent amount of research under my belt, and plenty of letters of recommendation. With my grandmother gone, I hadn't hesitated to take the offer, to sell the house I'd grown up in.

My life had been pathetically empty.

So, no, it hadn't taken long for KTS to become my family, and the driver was right, I would never, *ever* betray them.

"I could," the passenger said moodily. "I love her."

Biting back a *what the ever-loving fuck* (because how could a man love me without me knowing?) I slit my eyes, carefully trying to see without giving anything away, but outside the car, night had fallen, so I couldn't get a clear view.

Although, something I *could* see was there were no lights around, telling me that we weren't anywhere near civilization. Fuck. So running off and finding a phone nearby was off the table, and hiding until someone hopefully located me and sent in the cavalry to save the day was my plan.

Let it be noted that I didn't like this plan.

Tough shit, Ollie. Or maybe, suck it up, buttercup was just as effective. Either way, I kept my eyes barely open as I searched for anything that might be used as a weapon, and not finding any, I continued to take stock. I was just in my sweats and hoodie, but I had sneakers on. They, unfortunately, weren't my boots with the hidden blade in the sole, so I wouldn't be able to use the knife to cut my hands free.

But there were plenty of techniques to snap the plastic restraints, and I'd been taught each and every one. If I could get far enough away, I could get my hands loose. My legs weren't bound, so that was a plus, though my knee was throbbing in a way that told me running would make me very unhappy in the morning.

Still, I'd take an angry knee and being alive to the alternative.

"You didn't have a chance in hell in convincing her to join the Society, and you know it." The driver sighed. "Now, I'm going to have to shoulder your shit and clean up your fucking mess."

"You're not killing her," the passenger said.

"Then *you* are," the driver retorted. "But either way, this bitch isn't going back with us. You put the bullet in her head, or I do."

"That's not fucking happening!" the passenger shouted. "She's coming with me. They *promised* she would come with me."

"Hey! Fuck off!"

I opened my eyes fully to see the passenger, his body and face covered in shadows, reach for the steering wheel. The men scuffled, cursing and yelling, and then the passenger got his hands on the wheel. The car swerved, tires squealing on the pavement, and I dug my toes into the door, pressed my back into the seat so I didn't fly onto the floor as it screeched to a halt.

"Fucking asshole!" The driver shifted and shoved the passenger back and—

Bang.

One gunshot, and the passenger slumped into the seat.

One more, and I knew he was gone, along with us having any hope of learning what the Society was and how many of KTS's protected secrets he'd given them.

Then the driver turned toward me, and when I saw his face, it confirmed what I'd already suspected.

Daniel lifted the gun.

I kept my eyes open now, didn't bother to hide, but I did try to make myself as small of a target as possible.

His finger curled back, and now I shut my eyes, waited for the searing agony of a bullet tearing through my skin—

Honk!

The blare of a horn.

The shriek of brakes.

Then both were drowned out by a deafening *crunch.*

I heard the gun go off as my body was thrown forward, colliding with the seats in front of me, the center console crashing against my ribs, sending pain lancing through my torso. I bit back my cry of pain, forced my body to stay limp and rolled with the impact, lying still for one moment to suck in air.

Then I slit open my eyes, blinked against the bright lights shining through the window, and reached for the door handle.

It didn't budge.

I wriggled to my knees, yanked the handle, once, twice more. Then I managed to wedge it open, to start to squeeze my way out.

"I-I—let me help."

I looked up, saw a young teenage boy with blood dripping down his temple reach for the door. He pulled it back enough for me to slip free.

"If your vehicle is drivable," I said, "get in it, and get the hell out of here."

"I'm—I'm so sorry," he said. "It's dark, and your l-lights were off. The car was in the m-middle of the road"—he waved a hand, the bright lights of his SUV showing that Daniel indeed hadn't bothered to turn his on, and that the tussle over the steering wheel had drawn the sedan to a halt in the middle of the dark, secluded road—"I didn't see you. I—I—"

I grabbed the boy's hands in both of my bound ones. "It's not your fault," I said. "But you need to go."

He blinked, eyes going to my wrists then back to mine. "You're tied up."

I nodded, dropped his hands, and nudged him toward his car. "Honey, you need to get out of here."

The kid stared at me, mouth agape. "But you're bleeding."

"So are you."

He lifted his fingers to his temple, going pale when he saw the blood, wavering on his feet.

"Focus," I ordered. "What's your name?"

"Dominic."

"Okay, Dominic, it's very important you listen to me," I said, making sure to hold his gaze. "It's not safe. You need to leave right now and get someplace safe."

"But you're—"

A groan had me glancing toward the driver's seat, and I saw Daniel stirring. "Fuck," I hissed, my side burning, my knee throbbing. I peeked in through the window but couldn't see the gun anywhere. Fucking perfect.

"A-are you okay?"

No, I wasn't.

This kid was in shock, and he needed to get away from Daniel.

"I'm fine." I turned back to Dominic, recognized he wasn't going to be capable of moving, so I took his arm with my bound hands and dragged him back toward his car. "See if you can drive it, and go to the police, the sheriff, just get your ass some-place safe."

He got in, turned the key.

Nothing happened.

Fuck.

He got back out.

"Run," I hissed. "Get the hell away from here. Get some-place safe and call the police."

"I've got to get my bag."

Another groan, movement in the car.

And I knew *I* had to move, had to get this kid moving, to put some distance between him and Daniel. Because I knew that once Daniel was conscious, he wouldn't hesitate to snuff out Dominic's life. A man like Daniel didn't give a shit who he took down. If someone was in his way, they were easy collateral damage.

"Here."

I glanced back, saw Dominic had emerged, backpack in hand. He held up a pair of scissors.

"Thanks," I said and quickly held my arms up. He snipped, and I was free. "You got pen and paper in there?"

The boy nodded, pulled them out.

I wrote Laila's cell on it. "You get to a phone. You call this number, and you tell them that you've seen Olive—" I looked around for landmarks to pass on in case my tracker was malfunctioning—

"I know where we are." Dominic named the highway, then pointed behind me. "Mile marker twenty-two."

"Good," I said. "Tell them that. Now, go—"

"Bitch!"

I turned, saw that Daniel had straightened in the car, eyes arrowing straight for me.

And, of course, the fucker had the gun.

"Run!"

Finally, Dominic was unstuck enough to run.

Daniel fired.

But the glass was bulletproof and so it didn't penetrate. Though the impact of the gun firing had made the glass splinter, the panel held, and I chanced a glance over my shoulder to see that Dominic had disappeared.

Good.

I ran the other direction, straight for the tree line, straight for cover, and as fast as I could manage. There were probably snakes in these fucking woods or poison oak or ivy or sumac, or whatever hell-inducing, rash-giving plants were native to these parts that I was running right through, but I'd take a rash over a bullet any day. Though, I'd like to avoid the snakes, or at least the venomous ones, because they'd kill me just as easily as Daniel.

Regardless of any of that, I ran straight out from the road as quickly as I could, leaving my path obvious and easy to follow until I hit a creek.

Then I used that to disguise my circling back.

Because backup was coming to mile marker twenty-two, and I needed to be close enough to be ready for it.

"I know you're out here, you fucking bitch!"

I wondered how late it was. How long I'd been unconscious. How far from base I was. I tried to do all sorts of mental calculations to figure out how long I needed to hide out here.

But I didn't *know* enough. There were too many variables, and as I heard Daniel's footsteps getting closer, I worried that my plan to circle back had been incredibly stupid. I should have kept with putting distance between us, because he had the gun, and I had absolutely nothing with which to protect myself.

I hadn't even found a big log I could bash him over the head with.

Quietly, I crept forward, moving up into the brush near the embankment, using the muted moonlight overhead to scan for Daniel.

But the man had gone quiet, along with his footsteps.

I hardly breathed, my ears straining to hear any sound of his approach. It was too quiet, not even a bird or the sound of the insects to break it.

And I knew that meant he was close.

Too fucking close.

I needed to move and do it quickly. Otherwise, I was a sitting duck out here. Carefully curling my toes beneath me, I prepared to bolt.

And that was when I felt the cold barrel of the gun at the base of my neck.

CHAPTER EIGHTEEN

KTS Satellite Base
Western Georgia
22:52hrs

Linc

"Fucking bastard," I said, staring at the screen as the pieces fell into place.

Is had led to Tom's reports, which had then led to a flurry of activity to discover who might have access and the ability to change the report.

And one-by-one, I crossed people off the list.

Until only one remained.

I looked up at Laila, whose face clouded with anger. "Fucking bastard."

Hannah, on the other hand, was already moving, though her words were clipped with fury. "We've got to get to his lab."

I stood up so fast the chair tipped over backward, and I ran out of the room. I didn't stop for weapons or wait for backup. Any of my typical planning and plotting weren't on the table.

I had to get to the bastard.

I had to get to . . . Jack.

Jack, my teammate. Jack, a man who'd saved my ass more times than I could count.

And Jack, the only agent who'd had the technical know-how, the clearance, and the ability to manipulate Tom's report.

The only one who had the skill to erase camera footage, who could clear keypad data, could alter card readers, and who could do it easily, seeing as he was the one who'd implemented the system in the first place.

No wonder we hadn't discovered anything from the day of the bombing.

He'd hidden and erased anything that might have pointed us in the direction of the traitor—pointed at him.

As I ran, I remembered how he'd shown up after everyone today, how he'd responded after the rest of my team had already appeared at Hannah's S.O.S., how he'd been the last to show up on the day of the bombing, hadn't checked in afterward. I remembered the look in his eyes when I was with Olive, the comments, the ones I'd taken as teasing, but I now realized had been laced with darker meaning.

He was fucking neck-deep in this, and he'd taken Olive.

Fury filling my every cell, I swore to fucking God that the moment I got her back (because I wasn't allowing my mind to consider the possibility of anything else), I was going to kill the motherfucker.

He'd hurt Olive. Twice. Scared her. Twice.

Too bad I couldn't kill the fucker *twice*.

I jabbed my pin into keypads, barreled through doors, and then forced myself to slow as I approached the lab, trying to think, to plan—

Then just as quickly, I realized that wasn't going to happen.

I sprinted forward again, kicked open the door, and—

The explosion threw me back against the opposite wall.

"Linc!" Hannah yelled.

I barely heard her over the ringing in my ears, the lingering rush of the explosion. Fire had engulfed the interior of the lab, was licking along the tables even as the sprinklers kicked on.

Hannah grabbed an extinguisher from the wall and raced into the room. I grabbed the fire blanket out of the case next to it, did my best to smother the flames, and we were quickly joined by Dan, Jesse, Ryker, and Laila, all of us working as rapidly as we could to stop the fire from spreading.

We were all coughing by the time the worst of it was out, and my eyes stung like hell. Not to mention the pounding in my head, the cuts covering my arms, the burns on my hands.

And I couldn't fucking hear.

Or not much, anyway. The ringing was loud, made Hannah's words barely discernible.

"Out," she ordered, nodding to the hall.

I surveyed the room, seeing that the sprinklers could handle the rest, along with the other agents who had responded to the alarm, and stepped out into the hall. Lily ran up to me and immediately made me sit down, checking my pupils, shoving an oxygen mask on my face.

But when I went to tear it off, to stand up and continue searching for something, to find some way to figure out where he was—maybe Jack's tracker was working, or maybe—she grabbed my shoulder, forced me back down. "Sit, Linc. Now."

I would have protested, but at that moment I heard Laila snap, "Who the fuck is this?"

Lily and I both turned to look, saw the statuesque blonde's face go pale.

"Where?" A beat. "How long ago?"

This time, when I started to tear the mask off, Lily let me.

Laila's eyes met mine. "Gear on. Now. Garage in five."

Ryker and Laila sprinted in one direction, Jesse, Lily, and I took off in the other, followed by Dan and Hannah, stopping by the staging area to grab weapons and first aid supplies, working in rapid, efficient movements. Less than five minutes later, we were piling into the SUV, buckling in and prepping to tear out of the lot when Laila, Ryker, and Ava ran in.

I opened my mouth to protest, the doctor in me knowing she shouldn't be running on that broken ankle, but she put up a hand.

"Yell at me later," she said and got in the front seat, slamming the door behind her.

Laila jumped in the back, Ryker in the driver's seat.

And we were off, tires squealing as we emerged from the underground garage.

Unlike a normal mission, there was absolutely no chatter in the car, no noise except the ringing in my ears, the sound of Laila's clipped directions, and Ava checking and rechecking her sniper rifle as she assembled it.

It lay in her lap when Laila announced, "Park here," she ordered. "Ten minutes. Full sprint."

We piled out of the SUV, shouldered our packs, and followed Laila as she led us at a sharp clip down the road, though our boots didn't pound. Even with her cast, Ava's footsteps were barely audible, though she was trailing behind us significantly. Still, we'd been trained to move silently, and even though the ringing in my ears was only slowly fading, even though I could feel blood oozing down my arms, my chest, my right leg, I didn't slow, didn't move any different than normal.

Adrenaline and that training forced the majority of it to disappear.

Worry for Olive made anything else going on with me insignificant.

Heart pounding, lungs burning, I halted when Laila lifted a fist, studied the hand signals she gave, and then nodded, taking off through the undergrowth in order to follow the order.

Dan came with me, Ava limping up behind us.

"Go," she hissed. "I'll hunker down and cover your asses."

Dan nodded, stroked a finger down her cheek.

And then we were moving again, creeping through the undergrowth and closing in on the bright lights in the distance.

CHAPTER NINETEEN

Unknown location
Unknown hrs

Olive

"Up." The barrel of the gun pressed more firmly to the base of my skull. "Now."

Slowly, I pushed to my feet.

"Hands up." Another jab of that barrel. "Walk."

He should have killed me.

If what he'd said in the car was any indication, the moment he'd had a clear shot, he should have ended me.

That he didn't . . . well, on one hand, that boded ill for me. It meant he'd thought of a use for me, and I really didn't want to be useful to this man. On the other, it gave me a chance, so perhaps it boded *well*. Especially when that opportunity become slightly *more* than a mere chance as I crawled over a log and felt a pinch in my thigh. My gaze slanted down, saw the present Dominic had somehow left me. A present that might give me a chance to get the hell out of this.

"Keep moving," Daniel snapped, pushing me forward and nearly making me trip.

I played it up, staggering, limping heavily on my injured knee. "I'm dizzy."

"I don't fucking care." He shoved me again and this time, I let it take me down, catching myself on my hands, swiping the left one into my pocket as he roughly yanked me back up. "Keep moving."

Now that I had palmed the small pair of scissors Dominic had somehow left in my pocket, I did just that, walking the rest of the distance between the undergrowth and the road weaving through it. My knee still throbbed, but despite my limping, I knew the injury wasn't significant—it was more bruise than sprain or break. In the road, the lights from Dominic's car were still on, illuminating the area like a spotlight on a Hollywood set, and as I made my way back onto the road, I saw what I'd been trying to ignore earlier—Jack's dead body in the passenger's seat.

First Daniel, and now Jack. Who knew how far this went, how deep the rot at KTS had burrowed? All I knew was that it wasn't fucking good.

Jack had always seemed like a good guy, a little quiet, certainly, but never would I have suspected that he might turn against the agency and put agents' lives at risk. And I sure as shit wouldn't have ever expected him to drag me along with it, to declare some weird sort of unrequited love for me. I didn't even remember him asking me out or showing the least bit of interest in me as a woman. I couldn't even pinpoint the last time we'd spoken before that morning.

And now he was dead.

And we would never have the answer to why he'd gone rogue, why he'd thought to drag me with him, to what else he'd done to the base's electronics.

If he could alter reports, erase security footage and keycard information, he could do a lot of damage.

A lot.

But that would have to be handled later.

Daniel grabbed my shoulder, yanked me to a halt, the gun back at my nape and resting there long enough that I felt a cold bead of fear trail through me.

I pushed it down, thought fast.

"KTS is probably already closing in," I said. "They'll be able to track me."

Daniel snorted. "You mean with that little chip implanted in your arm?"

I didn't confirm or deny that.

"No." Daniel sneered when I didn't speak. "They won't be able to find you. That dumbass"—he nodded toward Jack in the car—"did one good thing. He had a backdoor into the chips. None of them will work for the foreseeable future."

Well, fuck.

I had to hope that Dominic had made it to a phone.

"What do you want?" I asked.

Daniel moved in front of me, the gun pointed at my chest. "Is this where you want me to go all evil genius and start spewing out my plan to take over the world?"

I shrugged. "That'd be nice, yeah."

He laughed, and though his expression was amused, I didn't like the sound of his laughter. Not at all. It was wrong, as though there were something broken inside this man. Something that couldn't be fixed. "I'll give you the TL;DR, Ms. Prim and Proper. It's not complicated." He leaned close. "It's for the *money*."

I stopped myself from tilting back, just barely. "No."

A frown turning the pretty-boy features of his face into a chilling rendition of what had once been beautiful but was now just filled with darkness. "No?" he asked, arching one brow.

"No," I said again, mind spinning, trying to keep that gun from firing. As I was struggling to say something, I caught a flicker out of the corner of my eye, behind Daniel's right shoulder. It might have been nothing . . . or it might have been a flicker of blond hair. Either way, I had to keep Daniel talking. "No," I repeated, louder. "If you were just after the money, you wouldn't have gone after Ava and Dan after they escaped. You would have taken your payoff for giving them up to the Mikhailova clan and Toscalo family, and you would have gone on your merry way." Another flicker, and I felt that deep pool of dread inside me relax slightly. That was definitely a flash of blond. "So no, this isn't about the money. This is about more than that."

He moved.

One second, he was sneering down at me, that creepy ass amusement on his face, and then in the next, his hand was wrapped around my throat, the gun was shoved against my jaw, and he was squeezing tight enough that black immediately crept into the edges of my vision.

"Bitch," he said, continuing to squeeze. "Fucking think you're going to play psychologist."

"It's true," I whispered. "Otherwise, you wouldn't be reacting like this."

"They fucking betrayed me"—his fingers tightened—"they deserve to hurt, just like I did."

"You were trafficking kids," Laila said, her long, blond ponytail hanging down her back.

Daniel froze, head whipping around to see his former team leader, the woman he'd risen up the ranks of the military with, the woman he'd been best friends with . . . until he'd betrayed her by doing exactly what they were hunting the bad guys down for doing.

"You sold them off to the highest bidder," she said, "and then you were selling the tapes of their sexual assaults." Laila's voice was quiet but absolutely deadly, a snake coiled to strike.

"Let her go."

Linc.

My heart sped up.

Daniel spun the other way.

"Just call it, Daniel," Ryker said, moving to stand next to Laila, drawing Daniel's focus again. "This is enough."

"Fuck you!" He whirled, yanking me back against his chest, the barrel of the gun sliding around my throat, not giving me an opportunity to break free. "It'll be enough when I say it's enough."

Dan appeared behind Linc, and the group of four took a step toward us.

The safety clicking off was loud in the quiet of the road.

"Don't," Daniel said, "Otherwise, she'll end up like him."

Four pairs of eyes flicked to the car, to Jack in the front seat. To Jack *dead* in the front seat.

"So, you're going to back the fuck up, you're going to tell me where your SUV is, and then I'm going to take it." The gun dug deeper. "And only when I'm free and clear will I let this bitch go."

Another *click*.

Only this time, it wasn't from Daniel's gun.

Instead, it was from behind him.

"First," a female voice said. "She's not a bitch. And second, you're not getting out of here alive."

He rotated us to face Hannah, with Jesse a step behind her.

My head began funneling through possibilities. We had the numbers, now we just needed the opportunity.

The metal of the scissors' blades had warmed where they rested against my palm.

"I can shoot her a hell of a lot faster than you can shoot me."

"Maybe."

A bullet flew over our heads, close enough that I felt the heat of it, felt my hair rustle as it shot by.

Hannah grinned. "But I'm not the one with a sniper's rifle pointed at my head."

Daniel went stiff, whirled me back in the direction of where the bullet had come from, using me as a human shield.

"You know that Ava can make that shot," Laila murmured, coming a step closer.

I felt Linc and Dan close in, too.

"She's not injured this time, and she's got plenty of ammo," Laila cajoled.

Daniel was still motionless, still stiff, still frozen. Then he exhaled . . . and the gun at my jaw dropped slightly away.

And I knew I had my opportunity.

I plunged the scissors into his thigh and dropped like a stone.

The gun went off, the shot blasting through the air, making my ears ring, but I didn't pay it any mind. I hit the ground hard, rolled to put distance between us just as another shot went off.

Daniel grunted, went down on one knee.

Hands grabbed my arm, yanked me away, Linc's scent filling my nose, his words almost indecipherable.

Then the air changed.

I didn't know how else to describe it, except to say that it was as though the very marrow of my bones froze.

"Fuck!" Linc.

Daniel had pulled something from his pocket, was pressing down on it.

Another gunshot.

Then—

Boom!

I felt more than heard it, the explosion renting the air, making my organs vibrate from the force of it. Linc's body came down on mine hard, pressing us both into the pavement as heat seared through the space over us. Then the noise came. A roar filling the quiet forest, bright light blinding me, making my lids squeeze shut.

And then . . . silence.

"Linc?" I whispered.

He lifted his head but didn't loosen his grip on me. "You're okay."

I nodded. "Are you?"

He nodded.

He *looked* like hell, cuts dotting the parts of him I could see, a bruise across his cheek, a burn on his forehead, but he appeared otherwise uninjured. "Thanks for the rescue."

His face softened, and he cupped my cheek with one hand. "I love you."

My mouth fell open.

I. Love. You.

Just like that, after *all* that?

But even as I was processing the words, he was pushing back, finding his feet, and helping me to mine.

We both looked around, looked back at each other.

And then we moved.

I ran to Dan, who was unconscious on the ground. He groaned by the time I made it to him, his hand lifting to his temple and the cut there. "I'm fine," he said as I began examining him. "Go check on the others." After giving him one more once over, I stood and moved to Laila.

She was kneeling next to Ryker, blood dripping down her arm as she put pressure on his side. His skin was pale enough to make me uneasy, but despite the rather large gash below his ribs, he didn't appear to be critical. Lily appeared with her first aid kit, knelt beside them.

"I'm good," he said. "Go help Linc. Hannah was shot."

Laila nodded. "We've got him."

I moved toward Linc and Hannah, who was sprawled on the ground, a bullet wound in her thigh. Jesse was unconscious behind her, but her pulse was steady, and there were no visible wounds. She woke after I passed some smelling salts beneath her nose, blinking and slowly sitting up.

I turned back to Hannah. "Go after him, Linc," she was saying. "I'm fine."

She was the *least* fine of all of us. Her wound was gushing a lot of blood, and her pulse, when I took it, was thready. I yanked open Linc's pack, began pulling out items, handing them to him as he ignored her protests and started dressing the injury.

A tourniquet to slow the bleeding. One of my namesake bandages to help with the pain and clotting. Then two more when it soaked through the first.

"Go," she gritted. "He can't have gotten far with those scissors in his thigh."

I blinked.

She propped her shoulders beneath her, smirked up at me. "Nice one, by the way."

"Lie down," I told her.

"I'm fine. Go get—"

"Hannah," Linc snapped, and the tone was so unusual that Hannah froze, her words cutting off. I knew he shouldn't be talking to his commanding officer that way, but I also understood. This was his teammate, his family, and she was fucking bleeding out on the ground—or would be, anyway, if we didn't get it under control.

Daniel could fucking wait.

Hannah needed us right then.

"Lie down," I ordered again.

"I'm—"

But exactly how *not* fine she was seemed to hit her at that moment, her skin going very pale, her breath hitching.

I grabbed her shoulders, coaxed her to the ground, shoving my sweatshirt beneath her head.

And then I helped stabilize her, putting pressure over the wound, continuing to hand supplies to Linc as he needed them. But it wasn't looking good. Hannah was bleeding too fast. She needed to get to the infirmary, and she needed to be there sooner rather than later.

"Laila," I said, when my leader came over.

She took one look at my face, at the scene on the ground

then snagged the keys from Ryker and handed them to Lily, who took off running.

"We need to establish a perimeter," Hannah ground out, her skin deathly pale.

"Dan, Jesse, and I are on it," Laila assured her and moved away to do just that.

"Pop?" Linc's gray eyes came to mine. "What do you think?"

I knew what he was thinking. Because he saw the same thing I did. The gray cast to her skin, the blood still soaking through the bandages. The need to stop the bleeding. Preferably that would be in a clinic, with sterile materials and blood bags at the ready. Unfortunately, that wasn't always possible.

And this was one of those impossible times.

I nodded, held his gaze. "It's the only way."

Keeping one hand on Hannah's leg, I snagged Dan's pack, reaching in for his kit, grabbing an injector of morphine, and sticking it into Hannah before she could protest.

"Hey—"

She slumped over.

Then I thrust my hand back in, closed my fingers around the tube of pure clotting agent, and tossed it to Linc.

"Ready?" I asked as he got situated.

He nodded.

I reached for the tourniquet, twisted it tighter.

Linc pulled out his knife, disinfected it quickly.

Then he ripped off the bandages.

CHAPTER TWENTY

Middle of fucking nowhere
Western Georgia
Unknown hrs

Linc

THE MOMENT the bandages came free, the blood started gushing.

But I had to make the wound larger, had to get the clotting agent into the right spot.

I used the tip of my knife to widen the incision. More blood came, making Olive yank harder on the tourniquet and Hannah cry out in pain despite the morphine she'd just been given.

I knew I couldn't focus on that, not when I needed to get the clotting powder into the right spot. Otherwise, no matter how many bandages I wrapped around this leg, no matter how much pressure or how tight Olive made the tourniquet, the bleeding wouldn't get under control.

And Hannah couldn't afford to lose much more.

Olive kneeled on Hannah's leg, putting even more pressure then held up a flashlight so I could see as I worked, widening the wound, searching for the worst of it. But there was so much blood, so much injured vasculature that all of it seemed to need it.

I knew that I couldn't go with that. I knew an artery had to be nicked, otherwise the other bandages would have done the job. So I resisted the urge to turn over the canister into the wound and kept searching.

Time was ticking.

The blood was pooling.

I knew I had to fucking do this, or Hannah would be—

"There!"

Olive shifted the flashlight beam, and I saw it, quickly squirting the canister's contents onto where the bleeding was the worst. It began working almost immediately, and I released a relieved breath, heard Olive do the same.

"Here," she said, shoving a bandage at me as I dispensed the rest of the solution.

I dropped the empty bottle on the ground, worked rapidly to wrap Hannah's leg, even as Olive kept moving while still putting pressure above the wound.

First, a shot of antibiotics. "Not exactly sanitary."

Then another bandage for me to wrap. "For extra security."

Then more morphine. "She's going to have a hell of a headache when she wakes up."

I finished wrapping Hannah's thigh, feeling the fist that had been gripping my gut finally loosen. "Did I tell you I love you?" I murmured, sitting back onto my heels.

Blue eyes that were darkened to navy in the night sky. "Yes, you did," she muttered. "And we're going to have a talk about your timing later."

I grinned then turned my focus back to Hannah.

She was still out, but her color seemed marginally less gray.

Olive stood, glanced around the clearing. I did the same, mentally checking everyone else, minus Lily, who was retrieving the SUV.

Laila, Ryker, Jesse, and Dan came over. "Okay?" Laila asked.

I nodded.

"Where's Ava?" I asked.

Dan's expression was stark. "She wasn't where we left her, and I tried her cell, but no answer."

Shit.

I opened my mouth, but before I could formulate a reply, Ava came jogging out of the woods, her stride clunky because of her cast, and hustled, as much as she was able,, over to Dan and Laila.

"I lost him," she announced darkly. "I trailed him through the woods, but even injured, he was faster than me." She glared at her cast, her expression thunderous. "I couldn't get a clear line of sight with all the trees. I did see he was picked up about two miles down the road. Nondescript black sedan. I got the plate, but I'm sure it'll turn out to be a fake."

There was a round of cursing, and then Lily drove up in the SUV, and we moved into action, quickly loading Hannah in the back, then the rest of us started to get in and buckled up.

But as I tried to herd Olive in before me, she stopped, glanced back at the car.

My eyes followed hers.

"Jack," she murmured.

I gazed over her head, saw Laila had heard her, and though a muscle ticked in her jaw and her eyes were furious, she nodded. "Dan and I will get him."

"Come on."

We crawled into the back next to Hannah, shifting so they could fit Jack's body in, and then Laila was behind the wheel, Ryker, Lily, Jesse, Ava, and Dan were buckled in, and we were driving away from the scene.

Lily had already called in a cleanup crew, but we couldn't wait.

Hannah needed the infirmary, and we still had a forty-five-minute drive.

"Will she make it?" Laila asked.

I was checking Hannah's pulse, trying to ignore Jack's dead body and the urge to open the hatch and shove him out the back. Her vitals were decent, though. Temperature and rhythm stable. Her skin slowly turning less gray. She needed blood and surgery to remove the bullet and suture up the damage, but she was stable for the moment. "She'll make it," I said, meeting her eyes in the rearview.

A nod.

The engine revving as she picked up the pace.

Turned out we could make the drive in only thirty-five minutes.

———

LATER, I found myself at a different woman's hospital bed, my eyes bleary, exhaustion dripping from absolutely every pore of my body, but confident that Hannah was going to pull through.

Part of me was seriously starting to hate this, though.

The waiting for a woman I cared about to wake up.

But we'd gotten Hannah to surgery, had removed the bullet fragments, cleaned and stitched the wound, and given her three pints of blood. Her skin was the proper color, she was being pumped full of antibiotics after our crude attempts at field surgery, and she was stable.

Now, I would just love it if she actually woke up.

Yeah, *that* would be good, and then maybe I wouldn't have nightmares of losing her mixing in with the nightmares of losing Olive.

That was more than any man could reasonably deal with.

Perhaps a little dramatic.

But after the panic that had gripped me in its talons so tightly for the last few hours, I figured I was allowed a *little* drama. It was certainly a safer alternative than attempting to lock these women in a padded room so they would never go out into the world and get hurt again.

"Okay," Olive said, coming through the room with a tray. "Your turn."

I put an arm around her waist, tugged her close to me, snagging the tray and putting it to the side. "I'm fine," I told her.

"Ah," she muttered. "The KTS catchphrase, and just what a doctor loves to hear."

"Pop," I began, coaxing her into my lap.

"Don't *Pop* me," she said, pushing against my chest and wriggling to her feet. "You don't let your teammates slide with the *I'm fine* bullshit, and I'm not going to let you slide with that, so don't even try it."

"I love you," I said.

Her eyes narrowed. "Also something that's not going to work with me," she muttered, reaching the tray and pulling on a pair of gloves. "Now, strip."

"Yes, take it off."

We both looked over at Hannah, relief pouring through me.

"How are you feeling?" Olive asked, moving to the pitcher on the counter and pouring a glass of water. She held it up to Hannah's mouth so she could drink.

"Just peachy," Hannah muttered after she'd sipped. "Now get out of here, lovebirds, I'm not dying today."

We both did a quick check of Hannah's vitals, which had her muttering about having to deal with two doctors rather than the usual one, and then we said our goodbyes, checking in with the nurse before we went.

"Don't think you got out of me cleaning those wounds." She rattled the tray she'd snagged from the room.

"I wouldn't dream of betting against you," I murmured. "My room or yours?"

"Yours," she said, and I immediately recognized the stupidity of my question. Of course, she wouldn't want to go back to hers, not with it being the sight of her kidnapping, not to mention it was trashed.

"Okay, baby," I said, snaking my arm around her waist.

"Thanks."

"You want to talk about it?"

She shrugged. "Not much to say. He surprised me outside my room, clocked me over the head as I was coming out to find you all and tell you what I'd discovered. I didn't even know who'd taken me until after he was dead." A shake of her head. "It was dark, and my vision was blurry, and the residual pain from the blow made it so . . ."

"What?"

Her face clouded. "He said he loved me."

I inhaled. "He did?"

Olive nodded, her hand rubbing over her face. "It's all so fucked up, and"—a sigh—"I swear to God, all I can think—and I know, sure as shit, that this shouldn't be *what* I'm thinking—is that Daniel called me Ms. Prim and Proper."

I froze. "What?"

"In the car, before I was able to place their voices. They were having a conversation about me, and Daniel said I was Ms. Prim and Proper." She pushed a hand through her hair. "Why the hell do I keep thinking about that? Of all the things I should be worrying about—Daniel out there, base security, considering Jack had his hands all in it, how deep or how many other agents are in this—and I'm upset that someone called me prim and proper."

I brushed my fingers over her cheek, a light stroke that made her eyes slide closed. "Clearly, he never saw you in those see-through sweats."

Her lips parted, outrage in her eyes.

And I prepared for a blast of anger. After what had happened, now that all the adrenaline was fading, it wouldn't be unexpected.

Instead, she blew out a breath.

Then laughter filled the air.

"Oh, Linc," she said. "I really want to tell you that I love you right now." Her blue eyes were dancing.

My heart squeezed tight. "Why don't you?"

She turned in my arms, the tray of supplies digging into my side, her free hand resting on my shoulder. "Because you said it in the heat of the moment and . . ."

"I might not mean it?"

One shoulder lifted. Dropped.

"What about Hannah's hospital room? That was the heat of the moment, too?"

Her lips turned up. "Obviously."

I drew her closer. "What about now?"

"Definitely."

"I love you," I said again.

"And circling back to still in the heat of the moment."

I chuckled, drew her away from me, and started walking again. "You're going to torture me with this, aren't you?"

She grinned, shrugged. "What do you think?"

I groaned. "Good God, you're going to be the death of me."

Olive spun so fast that I hardly processed the movement, and it wasn't until my back was against the wall, the air squeezed out of my lungs in an *oof* that I fully realized she'd moved. "Don't say that," she said, that tray clattering to the floor, the supplies fanning out in all directions. Her hands came to my shoulders. "Don't you dare say that. I *cannot* envision a world without you in it." A shuddering breath, her lips coming to mine. "You're mine, Linc. You became mine the moment you saved my life. You stayed mine when you took care of me. You're my family now, baby, and I don't want to ever imagine a world where you are not part of mine."

"Baby," I whispered.

"I was scared," she said. "But I knew you were going to come. I knew the teams would come. I also knew that I just needed one opportunity, and you guys would figure out how to get me out."

I rested my hand on the side of her neck. "You were right." My forehead came to hers. "We also owe Tom for the assist."

She smiled. "Sometimes routine is good."

"Say that to him."

Her head lifted, brows drawing together. "Why?"

"That'll be like porn to him," I said with a straight face. For the moment, anyway. Then she glared and I lost it, holding her to me and laughing into her shoulder.

She swatted at my chest, pushed me back. "You're terrible."

"Maybe." A beat. "But you're stuck with that terrible."

"Heaven help me." But her tone was light and as she bent to pick up the dropped supplies, I crouched to help her. Then we started walking back to my room again.

"Linc?" she asked as we approached the door. Her teeth were nibbling into her bottom lip, concern creeping back into those pretty blue eyes.

I smiled. I knew she was going to circle back to that list of concerns from earlier. "Yes, he is still out there, but you know as well as I do that none of us will stop looking for him. Base security has been tearing out systems and going back to square one, with increased foot patrols instead of relying on the camera, pins, and cards Jack put in place." I tucked her hair behind her ear. "And we can't worry if other agents turned. This is our family. It needs to be our safe place, and we can't start accusing people, especially when it seems like the majority of them are innocent."

"Linc—"

I cupped her jaw. "We'll keep our eyes peeled, of course. We'll track down anyone with a connection to Jack, ferret out any rot at KTS, but—"

"*Linc.*"

I stopped, glanced down. "What, baby?"

She gave me a smile that took my breath away. "I was just going to say, I love you."

CHAPTER TWENTY-ONE

KTS Satellite Base
Western Georgia
03:17hrs

Olive

THE WORDS HAD BARELY TUMBLED from my lips before Linc had me through the door to his room, the tray of supplies landing somewhere with a clatter, the heavy panel slamming shut.

Then his lips were on mine.

"You love me?" he asked after a long moment, his fingers having drifted to my waist and gripping me tight.

I was panting, my lips tingling, my thighs trembling. "You knew that already."

Dark gray eyes on mine, a mouth a hairsbreadth away. "Say it again."

"Why?"

He scooped me up, nipped my bottom lip. "Sass. Always fucking sass."

I laughed, clung to his shoulders as he carried me across the room and dumped me on the bed. "You love the sass."

"I love *you*."

My fingers found his jaw, the bristles on his skin the sweetest abrasion. "I love you, Lincoln MacFayden."

He inhaled sharply, his eyes going the slightest bit damp, and then he held my face in his hands and stared down at me. I could feel his love, *actually* feel it, as though it were stroking my skin, sinking into my body, being absorbed into my cells, my heart. And for a long moment, we stared at each other, just stared in a way that should have been creepy, but instead was . . . as though we were sharing every single thought in our minds, every feeling in our hearts.

I placed my hand over his chest, felt his heart thundering beneath it. "I love you," I said again, "but you're still not getting out of me cleaning those wounds."

A quirk of his lips.

Then he tolerated me cleaning him up.

Mostly because it involved undressing him.

First a shower, the two of us squeezed into the tiny stall, the steam gathering around our bodies, his erection hard and pressed to my spine as he ran soap over my body and gently shampooed my hair, his touch a bare feather of a stroke when he found the lump on the back of my head from Jack striking me, the plethora of bruises and abrasions from the crash and my flee through the woods.

"Your wrists," he murmured, and I glanced down to see the bright red marks. I'd cleaned them earlier, same as Linc had scrubbed out the cuts on his hands and arms before we'd assisted Lily with the surgery on Hannah's leg.

We hadn't needed to be there. Lily certainly was capable enough to complete the procedure with assistance from one of the other team's doctors and the nursing staff.

But it hadn't even crossed my mind to *not* be there.

Get clean, keep her safe, make sure the surgery went well.

Make certain she was out of the woods, and then we could rest.

It was our way.

"It's nothing," I said, slipping my hands from his grip and turning to face him. "They don't hurt."

He snagged them again, lifted them to his mouth, gently pressing kisses to the abraded skin. "I'm sorry I wasn't there."

I froze. "What the hell are you talking about?"

Regret filled his gray eyes, darkening them until they resembled storm clouds. "I shouldn't have left you alone." He shook his head. "If I'd been there—"

I placed a finger over his lips. "What are you doing right now? This wasn't your fault in any way, baby." But that regret didn't fade, and I knew it wouldn't fade with just one conversation. I'd seen it often enough with those I'd cared for over the years. Guilt for not being in the right place at the right time. Guilt for surviving. Guilt for not being able to stop something they couldn't predict.

And I saw it now in Linc's gaze.

I saw it in the way he gently kissed my finger then the marks on my wrists again. In the way he held me close, cradled against his chest, hands moving slowly up and down my back.

I knew it would take time for that wound to heal, that it would persist much longer than those on his body.

"You didn't know Jack was involved, honey," I whispered. "None of us did."

"I should—" He broke off, shook his head. "It doesn't matter what the shoulds are." A sigh. "No one saw it, and now he's dead."

Resting my head against his chest, I whispered, "Yes, he is." I hugged him. "I'm sorry. I know you two were friends."

He sighed. "I trusted him with my back."

The anguish in that statement made my heart squeeze, my stomach coil itself into knots. "I know you did."

I wanted to find other words to say something else, to find a way to make that pain go away. But there was nothing I could say to make that happen. We'd all been betrayed, Linc and his team doubly so since they'd all worked so closely together. There would be hurt and anger, just like we had felt when Daniel had first betrayed us. I wasn't on Laila's team then, but the shadow of what he'd done—what he was *still* doing—hung heavy like a lodestone.

"I wanted to kill him," he whispered, his arms coming around me, holding me tight. "When I found out it was him, when we knew he was the one who'd taken you. I was prepared to fucking *end* him."

I waited, and when no more words came, I said, "But he was still your friend."

He nodded, his chin rubbing along the uninjured side of my head, the bristles catching in my hair. "Yeah, Pop. He was."

My arms squeezed tighter, and I just held him, knowing there wasn't anything else I could say, nothing I could do to take the pain away.

Except to be there.

Because he hadn't had that before.

Because his ex hadn't given him that.

Because *I* could.

We stayed like that under the stream until I felt goose bumps prickle on his skin and realized that I was the one beneath the water and Linc was hardly getting a trickle.

Taking care of me.

Again.

And it's funny, but I'd been on my own for so long that I hadn't ever expected to love the feeling of someone looking out for me—not just in the field like my team did, not like a friend or family member like Laila and company obviously did. But like a man, as someone who loved me in a non-platonic way.

Thinking of what I might need before I needed it.

Caring that I was comfortable and warm and happy.

I wasn't trying to say my friends didn't look out for me.

It was just . . . the way that Linc did it was completely differ-ent. He made me feel good, and I knew I'd do anything in my power to make him feel the same way. Which was why I spun us around, why I washed his hair and soaped his body. Why, when I was finished with that, I turned off the water and wrapped him in a towel before grabbing one for myself.

"Baby," he began, trying to hand it to me, to dry my hair.

"Let me," I whispered. "Let me."

He froze. Then he nodded and held still as I ran a towel through his hair, as I caught the water droplets on his back, his chest, his legs, and when he returned the favor, I held equally still as he wiped the remnants of our shower from my skin.

Once we were dry, I led him to the bed, and as I bandaged the worst of the cuts and burns, we talked about the day, about how Linc had discovered I was missing, had seen my room torn apart—something I hadn't been conscious for, but knowing that Jack had probably been looking for the un-doctored report, the list I'd been making (and crossing off) of suspects until I'd narrowed it down to one.

To Jack.

Linc told me how the team had come together, how Jack had joined the search late—probably hiding my body, though I did wonder how he managed to get me out without being seen.

"He must have had help getting me off property," I murmured.

"It's possible, but I don't think so," Linc said. "At least not that explicitly. We gave him the opportunity to take you out. We called the alert, and everyone gathered in the mess for search assignments. We practically gave him a clear path to get you out." A sigh. "I remember seeing him come in with wet hair, saying he'd come late because he'd been in the shower and missed the alert. But now . . ."

"It was probably cover," I agreed.

He nodded, then explained how Jack had been given my laptop—and I supposed he had taken the opportunity to delete what I'd been looking at—then how Tom had come to them, how they'd finally made the connection, and how they'd gone to confront Jack at his lab.

This was where I got really freaked out.

Because Linc told me about the bomb in the lab. "Was anyone hurt?"

He shook his head, dutifully lifted one arm when I tugged at it so I could better see the bruise blooming on his ribs, and I realized the abrasions and cuts and weren't from the confrontation and explosion in the road.

"No," he said. "I took the brunt of the blast—or I should say," he quickly added when concern had my stomach twisting and probably bled over to my face, "the door took most of it. Jack's lab is trashed, though. Water damage and extinguisher powder everywhere. And what isn't under one of those two substances, is burned beyond recognition."

I checked his pupils. "Did anyone evaluate you for a concussion?" I asked, tilted his head from side to side, palpating and searching for any injuries I might have missed. "Did you hit your head?"

Shit. Two explosions in one day. That wasn't good for anyone's brain, especially since he'd been so close to both of them—

"Baby." He snagged my arms.

"What?" I asked, breaking his hold and continuing my search. That explained the bruising on his side, but what about his back? The skin there was newly healed and could be easily damaged, especially with being subjected to two explosions—

"*Pop.*"

I froze, glanced down at his face, the sharp tone breaking through my fussing. "What?"

"If you keep fretting over today, keep running your hands over my body—"

"What?" I asked with narrowed eyes. "You'll do *what?*"

One dark brow rose. "If you keep worrying and touching me"—his hand skated up my side . . . my *naked* side, and I realized my towel had fallen open—"I'm not going to be responsible for my actions." His fingers drifted forward, running back and forth on the sensitive skin beneath my breasts. "And yes, love, before you ask again, Lily checked me right after the explosion in the lab." His gray eyes found mine. "I'm fine." Those fingers still moving. "In fact, I find that I'm great."

My lips twitched. "What's it with you and towels?"

"Me and *taking off* towels?" He waggled his brows. "The last time we were in this situation, I believe it was your fault."

An outraged gasp on my lips. "*My* fault? You seem to be the one with your hand on my breast."

He glanced down, smirked. "Huh. How'd that happen?"

I sighed but bent to rest my forehead against his. "We're going to be okay, aren't we?"

His hand cupped my cheek. "Yeah, Pop, we are."

I thought so, too.

Which was why I shelved the rest of the conversation, knowing that while we needed to have it at some point, that we also didn't need to rehash it all tonight. We had time, and we had each other.

"You know," I whispered, "you never did take me on that date."

"You know," he whispered back, "I had a whole plan for how to tell you I love you while on it."

"Mmm," I murmured, my lips moving closer to his, brushing his with my next words. "Did it involve flowers and candles and chocolates?"

His eyes sparked with humor. "It involved you and those see-through sweats." He lifted his head to murmur in my ear. "And the new set of underwear I bought you."

I laughed.

He didn't.

"Oh my God." My brows rose as I sat back on my heels. "You're not serious."

He grinned, shrugged.

"Oh my God. You *are* serious." I swatted at his arm. "Linc, tell me you didn't buy me underwear."

"Isn't that what boyfriends do? Buy their girlfriends nice things?"

I couldn't deny that was sweet. Except for the humor dancing across his expression. *That* made me suspicious. "Maybe."

His grin widened.

"So, why am I suddenly scared?"

Another shrug.

"*Linc*," I warned.

He curled up, capturing my mouth in a kiss that sent my pulse skittering, heat skating down my spine, my thighs clenching around his waist, the strip of cotton of his towel the only barrier between us. Then he set me to the side, pushed up from the bed, and crossed to the closet. His towel dropped to the floor, and I wholly enjoyed the view when he didn't bother picking it up.

God, the man's ass was just bitable.

"Stop staring," he tossed over his shoulder.

"Not a chance," I tossed back.

And then he was back, holding a small, wrapped box, pink floral paper topped by a silver bow.

I lifted a brow.

"Don't try to tell me it's too girly," he said, setting it on my lap and kissing my throat. "A girl who wears lace beneath combat fatigues isn't worried about someone thinking she's too girly."

"For the record," I said, carefully removing the bow. "I don't wear lace under my combat fatigues." I glanced up, met his eyes. "Cotton all the way, baby, because I'm *not* a fan of chafing."

He chuckled. "Okay, lace under sweatpants then."

I nodded. "That I'll take."

Then I tore the paper from the box, setting it next to the bow, and finally, I tugged off the lid to reveal what was inside.

And then I somehow fell in love with him even more.

"Seriously?" I snapped.

But I wasn't mad, or at least not mad at anything other than the fact that this man was going to make me cry. Because inside the box were four pairs of underwear. Which, I got, probably sounded a bit icky or presumptuous, as though he were trying to tempt me into sleeping with him—though, frankly, it wouldn't take much tempting. When it came to this man, I was a sure thing.

But he was going to make me cry because he'd given me a rainbow of hedgehog underwear.

Cotton underwear.

"I love you, Pop," he said when I just sat there and traced the adorable little spiny shapes. "Lace or cotton, combat boots or sweatpants, ordering me about or washing my hair in the shower." Fingers on my jaw, my throat. "I'm just so fucking lucky that you've let me keep you here." He touched his chest over his heart.

"And, for the record, I don't care if you go halfway across the world on a mission. I don't care if you have to go deep undercover and won't be back for weeks or months. I don't care if you're away. Because I'll be there for you when you get back." He cleared his throat, fingers convulsing lightly. "I didn't have that before, didn't trust that when I did all the things I just said—that when I went on a mission, I would have someone waiting there for *me*, someone who got how important our job is, someone who'd be waiting without rancor or irritation." His fingers tucked a strand of hair behind my ear. "But when I saw you in the hall after my mission, not pissed because I hadn't checked in, not angry that I was late . . . fuck, but the clarity hit me hard, baby."

I swallowed. Hard.

My eyes stung.

And he kept talking.

"I'd already known that I liked you. Already knew that you were so fucking smart and good at your job and beautiful and kind, but I hadn't really expected that kindness to extend to me, baby. I—" He broke off, shook his head. "And when it did . . ." His eyes burned into mine. "When it did, I knew you fucking owned my heart."

I swallowed hard again.

I lost the battle with tears, one sneaking down my cheek.

Then I tossed the box aside and kissed him with everything in my heart. "You've become my family," I whispered when we broke apart. "You're in so fucking deep, I don't think you'll ever be able to find your way out."

A brush of his mouth to mine. "Well, I don't want to," he grumbled.

My lips twitched at the surly tone. "Good, because you're stuck with me."

His arms wound around my middle, hauling me toward him until our bodies were pressed together. "Good," he whispered.

And then he kissed me again.

I went to bed that night—or morning, rather—with the man who loved me holding me tight, knowing that we might not have every bit of the future figured out, that our love might be new and fresh like the first flowers poking up in early spring, but that we would be okay.

Knowing that the love would grow and change, the future would sort itself out.

Because I had this man, and he had me right back.

And I knew that was all that mattered.

CHAPTER TWENTY-TWO

KTS Satellite Base
Western Georgia
14:25hrs

Linc

LATER THAT DAY, Olive, our respective teams, and I went back to the scene to comb through the road and the surrounding woods searching for any clues the cleanup team might have missed.

But aside from a receipt for a local gas station, a collection of beer bottles and candy wrappers, we didn't find anything that might lead us in the direction of where Daniel had gone.

I knew he'd creep up again, that his rot would reappear, would continue to seep into the agency.

I just didn't know when.

For now, though, we had bigger problems. We needed to look at our own house, needed to make sure our agents were clean. We also needed more effective security—or perhaps to move base locations, depending on how far down we had been compromised.

And based on Jack's involvement, that was pretty fucking deep.

Ava was standing next to Olive, the former in her cast and only here after a verbal battle with his woman, who'd been pissed as hell that Ava had run on the break and was trying to work today. She'd only relented when Ava had made it clear she was coming and would bring a fucking chair to properly rest her ankle as need be.

The chair had been nixed, but so had the trek through the woods, instead, she and Olive were inspecting the road.

"I don't understand how there aren't any scorch marks," Olive was saying, scrubbing her boot through a few remaining shards of glass. "That explosion took us all down, and I swear, I felt it reverberate through me like a bomb." A frown. "But none of us had injuries like a bomb." She rubbed her temple. "I can't even remember anything after the bright light."

"The device he activated was like a flash-bang," Ava said. "But quieter. I got a little dizzy when the light came through my scope, but by then I was already jumping up and trying to follow." She sighed. "He'd already shot Hannah when I made it close enough to track him. She was awake—so maybe she didn't get the full force of the stun?" A shake of her head. "I don't know. She told me to go after him, but I should have—"

Olive touched her arm. "You didn't know she was critical."

"I should have stayed, should have made sure." Ava's face was drawn. "If she'd died, it would have been on me."

"No," I said, moving forward and resting my arm around Olive's shoulders. "That was on Daniel. He's the one responsible. Him and Jack. If they hadn't tried to come after KTS, none of us would be here."

She nodded, but I knew it wasn't that easy.

There would be plenty of blame to share.

"I wish I'd been able to get a fucking shot off when I was tailing him." She glared down at her foot. "Can't wait until this fucking thing comes off."

"If it helps, I've decided I'm working on something to help with bone growth for my next project," Olive told her.

Ava made a face. "Oh, it helps all right."

"I'll remind you that the last invention was created in response to that time you were stabbed." Olive's lips curved. "You keep getting hurt and pretty soon the team and I'll have developed a cure for every ailment."

"I'll do my best—"

She whirled around, gun in her hand. Olive and I fanning out and matching her actions.

Because there was movement in the bushes.

And not on the side that our team was on.

"Show yourself," I ordered.

A branch, heavy with green leaves, shifted, and I saw a teenage boy appear.

I didn't lower my gun, and neither did Ava. We'd both seen too many people who appeared innocent turn out to be the opposite. But Olive *did* drop her gun, hurrying across the road. "Dominic!" she said, grabbing onto him and hauling him close.

He said something I couldn't hear, and she laughed, and though I moved closer, letting my gun drop to my side—seeing Ava do the same—I didn't put it back in my holster.

Laila came up behind me. "Who's that?"

"*Dominic*, apparently."

Olive stepped back, wrapped her fingers around the kid's arm, and dragged him forward. "This is Dominic," she said. "He's the one who called Laila for me last night." She smiled up at him. "And gave me the scissors. These are my friends Laila, Ryker, Dan, Ava, Lily, and Jesse, and this is my boyfriend, Linc."

The kid's gaze came to mine. "Hi," he whispered.

I relaxed. Marginally.

Clearly, he was the teenager who'd helped her out of the car, the one who'd cut off her bindings. But the relaxation was only marginal because there was something in this kid's eyes that prickled my senses.

And I wasn't proven wrong.

The next words that came out of his mouth were, "I need your help."

"What's the matter, honey?" Olive asked.

"They're going to kill me."

———

WE GOT the story back at base, after we'd searched Dominic for tracking chips, had disposed of his cell, and checked his backpack for anything that might show that he was trying to fuck us over.

But there wasn't anything on the kid besides some raggedy textbooks, a few notepads, and a couple of pens and pencils.

I thought he'd cry when I crunched his cell and launched it into the woods, but he hadn't complained, just sat there and let us search him and his belongings until we were satisfied that bringing him back with us was . . . if not safe, then at least a manageable risk.

"My mom is dating David."

He looked around, no doubt at the blank faces surrounding him at the conference room, eyes going to the camera set up in the corner to record the interview (old school since the whole system of cameras had already been removed).

"Who's David?" Olive asked gently.

"The man who was driving the car," he said. "The one who was trying to hurt you."

An almost tangible change in the room.

"Ah," Olive said, "we know him as Daniel. He's dating your mom?"

He nodded.

"Where's your mom now, Dom?" she asked. "Daniel really isn't safe. We should get her—"

He shook his head. "She's gone."

I sucked in a silent breath. Gone as in—

"I—I saw what he did to you," he whispered. "How he was going to shoot you, and then I just remember a flash an—and I woke up and it was quiet. The cars were still there, and blood was in the road, and I thought he'd . . ." Dom closed his eyes, opened them. "I ran back to my house—it's not far up the road, and my mom wasn't there. Her car was gone and—"

"Was it a . . ." Ava listed off the make and model of the sedan that had picked up Daniel the night before.

He nodded, hope creeping into his expression. "She didn't come back last night. I waited and waited, and I thought . . . well, I came back to the road, thought maybe . . . I don't know . . . that she couldn't get through because the cops had blocked the road or something. But everything was gone." He glanced at Olive, at me. "Have you guys seen her?"

Silence.

Then Olive covered his hand. "She picked up Daniel before we could get to him."

More silence.

Though this time it was like a fucking punch to the gut, because I couldn't get the hurt in the kid's eyes out of my head. It was like this was the final blow, that he'd been holding onto a slender thread of hope and it had just been snuffed out.

I knew the feeling.

I knew it too fucking well.

"She left me to get to him." It wasn't a question, Dom's tone laced with resignation. "She didn't care, just left me because . . . she's in some fucked up relationship with a man who treats her like shit."

I didn't want to push him, but we needed to circle back to the important parts. "Why did you say they were going to kill you?"

Dominic's eyes met mine. "They knew I helped you."

Olive released a breath. "Daniel saw you?"

"I don't know." He shoved his hand through his hair. "I think so? I mean, he must have seen me with you in the road."

A sigh. "I went back home after everything was cleaned up to wait for my mom, but she didn't show. Instead, these huge SUVs—kind of like the one we rode in here—pulled up, and they started searching the house."

His gaze went to his hands. "I hadn't even made it inside, was still walking through the woods next to the house when they screeched into the driveway, and for a moment, I almost went out to greet them. I thought maybe they were with you guys, but . . . something made me wait."

He inhaled sharply. "And then they came out and someone said, 'the kid isn't here.' And another was pissed, said that 'David needed to teach me a lesson for interfering.'" He looked up, pain in his eyes. "I didn't mean to hit the car. I didn't even know he was in it. It was dark and in the middle of the road and—"

"None of this is your fault, Dom," Olive said.

Bleak brown eyes. "My mom is with him."

"We're going to find Daniel," she promised.

He nodded, but that bleakness didn't go away.

"Do you have any family we can get you to?" Laila asked. "Someone far away who you might be able to stay with for a while?"

"No." A beat. "It's always just been my mom and me. I haven't even gone to school in two years." He inclined his head in the direction of the books. "Not since we moved here with David."

I looked at the cover, saw what I'd missed before. They were battered because the kid had borrowed them from the library.

Fucking hell.

"Have you slept?" I asked. "Or eaten since yesterday?"

Dominic shook his head.

"Right," I said and stood. "Food, bed, and then we'll figure the rest out later."

Laila lifted her brows but didn't protest, and neither did anyone else. Olive walked beside me as I brought Dominic to a set of rooms in a section of the base that was under constant surveillance. I knew he saw the guards, but he didn't protest, just walked in through the door I opened and thanked me when I said I'd bring food.

When Olive and I returned with a tray—I wasn't quite up to letting her out of my sight yet—Dominic was already asleep, so we left the tray on the desk, made sure that a guard would always be posted outside his door—I was sympathetic, not stupid—and made that guard promise to get word to us the moment he woke up.

Then we walked back to the conference room to join the conversation, to plan our next steps.

First, would be getting the base secure.

Next, would be tracking down Daniel, though that probably related back to the first.

Last, would be setting up a trap to draw in any other rogue agents.

Jesse and Lily would be in charge of the last. Laila and Ryker were on tracking down Daniel. Ava and Dan would be on base security. And Olive and I?

We were going to figure out what to do with Dominic.

EPILOGUE

Olive

I GLANCED up at the knock at the door to my office and smiled. "Dom, come in."

The lanky teenager slipped inside the room, closing the door behind him. "Hi, Ollie," he said, his voice as soft as ever. "Sorry to bother you."

It had been two months since Jack had kidnapped me. Two months minus one day since Dom had come to live on base.

Two months minus approximately two days since we'd run out of ideas of what to do with him. Foster care wasn't an option, not when the kid had already been through the wringer, and not when putting him into someone else's home might bring danger upon whatever family or group home that took him. Beyond the danger—also a factor in why we couldn't just set him up with some money and turn him loose—I felt responsible for him.

He'd helped me when he hadn't needed to.

And that had put him at risk.

So I'd gone up against the powers that be, going so far as to threaten to leave. KTS all together (luckily it hadn't come to that), and Dom had a place to stay here until it was safe for him to leave

And I was going to make sure that leaving didn't happen until *he* was ready to leave.

Then I still wouldn't let him go completely. Because he was family, too.

He was a good kid, and these last two months had shown that. He'd researched and found an online school to attend, was slowly getting caught up with what he'd missed and hadn't been able to supplement over the last couple of years. I'd bought him books and supplies, much to his protests and for which he'd stubbornly paid me back by going to the mess and picking up shifts washing dishes. And just last week, I saw that he'd somehow gotten another job mopping hallways.

And we still hadn't been able to locate his mom.

Or Daniel.

But his mom was more important to him, which was why he came in this time nearly every day asking me for details, if we'd had any sightings.

Which we hadn't.

Which I hated to tell him because I hated to be the one to make his eyes go sad. But I still told him, still gave him any information I could. Because I knew what it was like to be alone in the world, knew what it was like to be drifting without family.

Hopefully soon he would understand that he was part of mine.

"Looking for an update?" I asked.

To my surprise, he shook his head, his lips turning up at the corners, mischief entering his eyes, and he held up a letter. "I'm supposed to give you this." He thrust the envelope into my hands. "See you later, Ollie."

I blinked, looked around as though I expected someone to jump out because I was on a hidden camera show.

When no one appeared, I glanced down at the envelope.

Then recognized the handwriting.

"Oh, Linc," I muttered. "What did you do?"

Why don't you find out and open the envelope? I imagined him saying.

I listened to my imaginary boyfriend's command and tore the flap free, pulling out the note inside.

8pm. Your room. Dress nice.

I frowned.

Then I smiled.

Was tonight Date Night?

Linc had been talking a big game about this date he'd planned, lamenting over how nice it was going to be, whining about all his plotting going to waste because we'd been too busy with everything to sneak out for a date.

And then last week, when we'd been planning on dinner, my belongings had arrived from England—seeing as how Georgia was going to be my team's home base for now—and we'd spent our free night unpacking my stuff into Linc's rooms.

Because I had a live-in boyfriend.

Also, could I say how much I loved the fact that I hadn't even had to consider what I was going to do about a kid I was taking responsibility for in Georgia and a team based in England. They'd all just up and relocated to this base and wouldn't hear a word of my protests.

Smiling as I shut down my computer, I hurried from my office and made my way back to our rooms, seeing that it was almost 8:00 already and if my man wanted me to dress nice, it was going to have to be a quick change.

I was thinking I needed to train him better, to remind him

that makeup and hair took time and couldn't be materialized on a whim, when I turned the corner.

And saw him.

He was standing outside our rooms, a bouquet of vibrant purple and red flowers in his hands. He smiled, closed the distance between us, kissing me lightly on the lips.

"I'm not ready," I protested.

"I don't care," he said. "I was kidding about the dress nice part." Another kiss. "I just figured it would be the only way to get you out of your office in a timely manner."

"That's not true."

He lifted a brow.

"Okay, fine. It's probably true." I had been spending my days elbow-deep in bone chemistry. I was determined to find a way to heal them faster.

"Exactly." He kissed me again.

"Stop that," I ordered. "I need to get ready."

"And I told you," he said. "You don't."

"But it's Date Night."

One brow lifting. "Is it?"

I stomped a foot. "You're telling me the note isn't for Date Night?" I asked archly.

"I didn't say that."

My temper began to spike. "*Linc.*"

He smiled, tugged on my hair. Then he pressed the bouquet into my hands, opened the door, and nudged me inside. "It's Date Night," he murmured as I stumbled to a stop, taking in the sight.

Candles lined every flat surface, covered plates were placed on the table, silver domes ready to be lifted, soft music played in the background.

And more flowers.

So many flowers, the floral scent hit me just inside the door.

"We haven't had much luck in getting out for Date Night," he murmured. "So I thought I'd bring Date Night to us." A beat when I didn't respond, when I was so touched that I *couldn't* respond. "I promise, we'll get out for a real one soon."

I set the flowers down on the shelf near the door, spun, and launched myself into his arms.

"It's perfect," I whispered, kissing him long and slow.

"Wait until you see what's under the domes," he said, waggling his brows when we broke apart for air.

I laughed, but then he brought me over to the table, picked up the silver cover, and . . .

This *man.*

He'd discovered my favorites, and they were all there on my plate.

I dropped the dome onto the table, launched myself at him again, and kissed this man with every bit of love that I possessed for him. My hands going to his shirt, tugging it over his head, then to the button of his jeans, as his hands worked on getting off my clothes just as quickly.

We tumbled onto the bed, and I showed him how much I loved him.

"There are perks to an in-house Date Night," I murmured lazily, much later, as we lounged in bed and ate off the plates, a Gold hockey game on in the background.

"Why's that?" he asked, his fingers tracing light patterns on my naked thigh.

"Because I get to spend it with you," I said. "And just you." I cupped his cheek. "And that's more romantic to me than any restaurant."

His eyes got warm.

I felt his love deep in my soul.

And I knew we'd have many more in-house Date Nights in the future.

Fuck, I fucking loved this man.

A finger brushing along my nose, a murmured, "Distracted."

"Such a fucking pain in the ass," I grumbled, but I did it

laughing and hugging him tight, and then Linc spent the rest of the night *really* distracting me.

And I could hardly believe the curse words that came out of my mouth.

Worth it.

So worth it.

EPILOGUE
PART TWO

KTS Satellite Base
Western Georgia
06:58hrs

Jesse

I SIGHED and rubbed my eyes, the final part of my plan in place.

My teammate Lily and I had been working on ferreting out any remaining traitors at KTS.

We'd investigated every angle; we'd thought about every possibility.

And I still couldn't be sure that I'd considered them all.

There must be something I was missing, something that I could plan for, something . . . I wasn't going to find tonight because I was too freaking tired.

There was a knock at the door, and my eyes flicked up.

"Leo," I said, smiling, despite my fatigue. "When did you get into town?"

"Just tonight."

"That's awesome." My smile didn't fade. "It's really good to see you."

The agent, a member of my former team before I'd shifted gears and landed under the direction of my current commanding officer, Hannah, smiled back. "It's good to see you, too, Jess."

I nodded.

Waited.

He just stared at me.

Which was a problem. Because the man had the dreamiest green eyes I had ever seen. They were pools of blazing emerald, a shocking contrast to the deep olive of his skin. And his smile —that one he'd just unleashed on me—well, I wasn't a woman who swooned over a man, but this one? He'd always made me hyperaware of his presence, desperate to be more than friends with him.

But he'd been a teammate.

And further that, I was *me*.

I wasn't cute. I wasn't curvy. I was . . . strong.

I had broad shoulders and muscular thighs. I could program an explosive—or take one apart—in seconds to minutes, depending on how complicated they were, but I wasn't a woman who inspired a man to be attracted to her.

I was the funny friend.

The great buddy to hang out and have a beer with.

Which was fine. I loved myself, loved the strength I'd worked hard for. It was just . . . part of me wanted the romance, wanted the fancy dress, wanted the man who thought I was the most beautiful woman on the planet.

Well, everyone had their fantasies, and I wasn't immune, and in the meantime (because Leo *was* and would most definitely *always* be a fantasy), I'd focused all my energy on being a good agent, a good teammate, and a good friend, all in that order. Unfortunately, none of those attributes gave me any clue on how to proceed with this conversation.

"Um, did you need something?" I asked.

He shook his head.

I waited. Again.

Then he smiled. *Again.*

And heat coiled in my abdomen, my thighs clenched together. I could have sworn I smelled him from all the way across the room.

Then he crossed to me, tugged me up into his arms, and for one moment . . . *for one moment* I thought that perhaps the fantasy in my mind might be for real. That he was a heartbeat away from declaring that he had always loved me and then was going to swipe a hand across my desk, lay me across the table, and have his merry way with me.

But . . . fantasies.

Because that *one moment* passed.

He released me, stepped back, and punched me in the shoulder. Not lightly either, but hard, like one dude would punch another. It didn't hurt . . . not physically anyway. "I'm your new teammate, Jess!"

Then he punched me again.

And I felt my heart crack . . . just a little bit.

Because it had only been a fantasy. *Just* a fantasy.

And maybe if I kept telling myself that, it wouldn't hurt so much.

LEVELING THE FIELD

Jesse's story is coming June 14th, 2021!
Preorder at www.books2read.com/LevelingTheField

KTS SERIES

Prequel Novella
Fire and Ice (Hurt Anthology)

Full Length Books
Riding The Edge
Crossing The Line (March 22nd, 2021)
Leveling The Field (June 14th, 2021)

ALSO BY ELISE FABER

Billionaire's Club **(all stand alone)**

Bad Night Stand

Bad Breakup

Bad Husband

Bad Hookup

Bad Divorce

Bad Fiancé

Bad Boyfriend

Bad Blind Date

Bad Wedding

Bad Engagement

Bad Bridesmaid

Bad Swipe (June 28th, 2021)

Gold Hockey **(all stand alone)**

Blocked

Backhand

Boarding

Benched

Breakaway

Breakout

Checked

Coasting

Centered

Charging

Caged (April 12th, 2021)

***Breakers Hockey* (all stand alone)**

Broken (May 24th, 2021)

KTS Series

Fire and Ice (Hurt Anthology, stand alone)

Riding The Edge

Crossing The Line (March 22nd, 2021)

Leveling The Field (June 14th, 2021)

***Love, Action, Camera* (all stand alone)**

Dotted Line

Action Shot

Close-Up

End Scene

Meet Cute (April 5th, 2021)

***Love After Midnight* (all stand alone)**

Rum And Notes

Virgin Daiquiri

On The Rocks

Sex On The Seats (April 26th, 2021)

***Life Sucks Series* (all stand alone)**

Train Wreck

Hot Mess

Dumpster Fire

Clusterf*@k (August 16th, 2021)

***Roosevelt Ranch Series* (all stand alone, series complete)**

Disaster at Roosevelt Ranch

Heartbreak at Roosevelt Ranch

Collision at Roosevelt Ranch

Regret at Roosevelt Ranch

Desire at Roosevelt Ranch

Phoenix Series **(read in order)**

Phoenix Rising

Dark Phoenix

Phoenix Freed

Phoenix: LexTal Chronicles **(rereleasing soon, stand alone, Phoenix world)**

From Ashes

In Flames

To Smoke (October 18th, 2021)

Stand Alones

Someday, Maybe (YA)

ABOUT THE AUTHOR

USA Today bestselling author, Elise Faber, loves chocolate, Star Wars, Harry Potter, and hockey (the order depending on the day and how well her team -- the Sharks! -- are playing). She and her husband also play as much hockey as they can squeeze into their schedules, so much so that their typical date night is spent on the ice. Elise changes her hair color more often than some people change their socks, loves sparkly things, and is the mom to two exuberant boys. She lives in Northern California. Connect with her in her Facebook group, the Fabinators or find more information about her books at www.elisefaber.com.

[f] facebook.com / elisefaberauthor

[a] amazon.com / author / elisefaber

[BB] bookbub.com / profile / elise-faber

[O] instagram.com / elisefaber

[g] goodreads.com / elisefaber

[P] pinterest.com / elisefaberwrite